# Magnanimous Absolution

By Erik McGowan

Edited by Erica James

Cover design and formatting by Erik McGowan

Cover photo by Ganapathy Kumar

ISBN 978-1-7326545-0-1 (pbck.)

978-1-7326545-1-8 (ebook)

# Acknowledgments

**I would like to thank** - My Family, Ashley Williams, Azya Maxton Sherie Crawford, Josh Flowers, Jason Langdon, Andrew Herd, Norsha Roland, Alexis Skinner, Kelsey Williams, Joshua Camins, members of Baltimore Science Fiction Society (BSFS), Carl Allen, Whitney Cunningham, Tristen Webb, Chantel Roberts, S.Rasheem, and anyone else who, over the years have read my short stories, this very novel, or had given me some kind words that helped motivate me to continue and complete this dream.

## Special Thanks to:

Ashley Williams for putting up with my request for reviews on all of the shorts; the good and the bad ones, and this very novel.

My mother, Vicki McGowan-Smith, for being my alpha reader for most of the novel.

My brother, Derek M. McGowan, for allowing me to write two short stories for his novel and helping with the beta reading.

My sister, Nikkia Carter, for the boost in confidence while I was finishing this novel off.

My father, Derek M. McGowan Sr., for all of the feed back.

Thank you to Erica James, my first editor, for popping up at just the right moment when I was on the search for one.

# Table of Contents

Chapter One - The Legend                1

Chapter Two - Welcome...                9

Chapter Three - The Switch              15

Chapter Four - Early Career             33

Chapter Five - French Maid              53

Chapter Six - Humble Pie                70

Chapter Seven - The Maestro             81

Chapter Eight - New Blood               112

Chapter Nine - The Fall                 135

Chapter Ten - Last Day                  167

Chapter Eleven - Last Day Part II       180

Chapter Twelve - Editorial              203

# CHAPTER ONE

## The Legend

The deli's door swung open, agitating a tiny bell attached to the door frame. Its tone was loud enough to alert the employees of the four generation old delicatessen, but quiet enough not to disturb the average patron and their enjoyment. Almost in unison, a few of the employees said, "Welcome to—," but were cut off by the on-duty cashier. "It's just Frank," she said after glancing up.

Frank had been a customer of this well-established establishment since before his birth. His late mother would come there to get irregular sandwiches to satisfy her pregnancy cravings. As soon as he was old enough to chew, his mother would bring him along. Through the years, he had seen three generations of the original owner's family run the store. If it weren't for his cataracts, he would be able to see the fourth.

He stumbled in through the door, feeling his way to his favorite seat; a bar stool at the very end of the counter on the opposite end of the restaurant. The deli's layout was like a snapshot of history. Its design resembled 'A Boulevard of Broken Dreams' with booths and a more open floor plan. Each piece of its original furniture had some sort of makeshift repair. The stenciled flower patterns that previously brightened the tables with vibrant spring colors has long since faded. Some of the tables had small patches of the designs stripped all the way down to its hard plastic underneath. All of the stools on the other hand were new. The rest of the deli was accented with pictures of famous customers throughout the years and modern day appliances to keep up with the newer regulations.

As Frank wobbled to his seat, he bumped into some shoulders and stepped on toes. He apologized each time, but those apologies were only met with teeth sucking and under-the-breath curses. Halfway to his destination, Hazel, the previous manager, saved him from his bumbling.

"Oh, hello there," Frank said politely, confused by the hand guiding him along. It was soft and pleasant like the voice that followed.

"I got you, Frank," Hazel said. "Sit down right here." She patted on the top of the stool.

"Hazel." He smiled a toothless grin. He drew her in for a strong embrace.

Frank was excited to hear her voice again. Hazel had always been kind to him, and he has always tried to treat her the same. Frank had been like an uncle to her. He was at most of her biggest moments in life; when she celebrated her childhood birthdays, when she had her graduation parties, and all her days managing the deli. Recently, she hadn't been around as much since her nephew took over the deli about five years ago.

# MAGNANIMOUS ABSOLUTION

They spent a few minutes catching up before she took his order. He'd misplaced his dentures at home so he couldn't get his favorite, roasted turkey breast muffaletta. Instead, he asked for rice pudding without the raisins and an ice-cold ginger beer to wash it down.

Frank reached down to his fanny pack to grab some cash. It sat on his left hip so that he could reach it easier.

"You know it's on the house," Hazel said.

Frank smiled at her. His food has been on the house for over fifty years now. Ever since the original owner, he hasn't had to pay a dime. Hazel's nephew never liked that idea. The business has been struggling, and every bit of income was welcomed.

The door clanked against the bell again. Another customer, Mark, made his way into the deli. The employees started to say their normal greeting. "Welcome to—"

"Yeah, yeah," Mark said without breaking his stride. He walked to the second booth from the door, sat down, slid to the corner, and stretched his leg on the bench. There was another gentleman, Chaz, sitting on the other side of the table. He looked to be several years younger, but both men were the same age. They'd been friends since childhood, going to the same schools from kindergarten through high school, often in the same classes. That familiarity changed around the end of their senior year. That summer was the last time they got to spend a good amount of time with each other.

While Chaz was pushed by his father to go to college and 'finish up his education', Mark was forced into the workforce and life as an adult. By the time Mark became eighteen, he was spending most of his free time helping his parents with the family business. Once August hit, Chaz moved away for college and didn't return until after he had graduated. Twelve long years had passed, and both were inevitably changed.

Chaz found his wife, changed his major two times before settling on journalism, and became a pescatarian. Mark found nothing but stress and hard work through those years. Both of his parents died a couple of years after his graduation, leaving him with the family business to keep it afloat. Chaz didn't show up for the funerals, but Mark wasn't mad at him—he didn't go himself. Mark put all of his pain and grief into his work.

They finally met up for the first time three months ago, when Chaz returned to The City for a job at the local paper. The first meeting was awkward for them. Their conversations were filled with summaries of life events mixed with long spans of silence. It was almost as if they were speaking different languages. Their blue collar/white collar points of view on life were like oil and water, floating along the surface of shallow conversations that never quite fused with each other's life experiences.

That first meeting might have been their last time if they would've solely talked about recent events in their lives. But once they started reminiscing about their youth, they could see a glimpse of their old friend again. Their present selves stepped away to let their youth and memories shine. Since that day, they met in this deli twice a week to talk. The meet ups would normally occur on Mark's off days, Wednesday and Saturday. This time however, Chaz had something to tell him, and he couldn't wait until Wednesday.

"Did you order yet?" Mark said, never looking at Chaz. He slid the closest menu in front of him and began his search.

Chaz pushed a crumb-filled bread plate over the top of the menu Mark was reading. "I ate a half hour ago, ten minutes after you were supposed to show up," Chaz said, "and I drank your water."

"Good, I wasn't going to drink it anyway." He waved the waitress over that was passing by. "Let me get uh, your wings and fries with a ginger ale."

"Sure thing," she said, shifting over to Chaz. "Do you want anything else, honey?"

"Nope. I'm fine," Chaz said with a friendly grin. The waitress gave a polite smile back and then walked away. They watched her leave.

"If I was younger," Mark said.

"If I wasn't married."

They both laughed.

"So, what's the news?"

"You probably won't believe this," Chaz said, mouth wide, grinning like a child. He had been holding back his excitement for a while but the focus on the topic changed that. "I'm going to meet Mr. Marvelous."

"Am I supposed to know who that is?"

"Mr. Marvelous." He waited for Mark's eyes to light up. His face stayed stagnant. "You know, Mr. Marvelous."

"Say it one more time. I'll remember then."

"Look," Chaz pulled a newspaper clipping out of his pocket and held it in front of Mark's face. It was one of the clippings from his collection. Throughout elementary and middle school, Chaz

5

collected every article that he could find about Mr. Marvelous. Back then, he would try to share the album with Mark, but sometimes it was like pulling teeth. Mark was more interested in sports.

Mark looked at it for a couple of seconds trying to connect the dots. "Yeah," he said while nodding. "That's right, I remember that guy. So, you saw him?"

Chaz agreed.

"Around here?" He looked around the deli. "Walking?"

"Nope. I got a letter from him at work yesterday. It came in the mail a couple of weeks ago, but it was sitting in the slush pile."

Mark tilted his head. "Slush pile?"

"Yeah. It's basically—a slow news pile."

"Oh, ok."

"So, since that super blizzard," Chaz said with air quotes, "in the mid-west, the paper's focus has been on that story."

"And they let you of all people meet him first?" Mark scratched his face. "Oh, I get it. It's called the slow pile for people that aren't too bright. That way guys like you don't feel left out."

Right before Chaz could fire off his rebuttal, the waitress showed up. "Here you go, honey." She placed the plates of food on the table in front of Mark. "Do you need anything with it? Hot sauce or dipping sauce?"

"No. Thank you baby," Mark said with a smile.

"Well let me know if you change your mind," She said.

"Slow as in slow news cycle," Chaz said to get back on topic.

"She forgot my ginger ale. If she wasn't so pretty..." Mark paused for a moment as he watched her switch back to the kitchen. "I'm still going to give her a tip though." He took a whiff of the wings.

"Anyway," Chaz said. "While I was working Thursday night, the features editor told me to look through the pile to see if there was anything that could be used. That's how I came across this." Chaz reached into his satchel, pulled out a manila envelope, and placed it face up in the middle of the table. He smiled with an air of pride and accomplishment.

"What's this," Mark said with a mouth full of chicken. He reached out to grasp the envelope.

"Are you crazy?" Chaz snatched the envelope back. "You're going to get grease all over it. Wipe your hands first."

"You right." Mark used a napkin to wipe some condensation off the cup and then used the napkin to clean his hands. "See, all clean," he said. "Now, hand it over." He snatched it out of Chaz's grip.

Chaz watched in horror as Mark fumbled through the envelope as aggressively as he took it from him. Mark pulled out the letter and looked over it for a few seconds. The whole thing was printed on two pages of white paper. His brow curled up with focus as he flipped through the pages. "That's it?"

"Yeah. What do you think?"

"I don't know, I didn't really read it." He shrugged. "I skimmed over it." Mark tossed the pages back over the table to Chaz.

"What is wrong with you? It's only two pages," Chaz said.

"Yeah, yeah. Just give me the gist of it," Mark said before returning to his food, stuffing his mouth with fries.

Chaz sighed. He then reached over grabbing the envelope and reinserted the letter with extreme care. "The first page is a bunch of articles and references to him. I think he was trying to make it like a puzzle of some kind. The last page reads,"

**I've been keeping up with your career. If you want to be the first to the greatest story you've ever heard, come see me.**

"with his signature, and his address at the bottom. I am going to go see him tomorrow."

"I thought you said you saw him."

Chaz shrugged. "I mean, I'm going to see him."

"What side is he on?"

"He's over by the east docks."

Mark leaned back. "The only thing over there are factories and The Loft. So, either that letter is fake, or he's going to have you hanging out at the dirty Loft." Mark laughed. "If he's in there tight with the locals, ask him if I can get a discount next time I stop through. Those girls can be pricey."

"It's not like that. I'm sure he is a changed man."

"Yeah. Tell that to Tracy," Mark said. "Hold up—maybe you shouldn't tell her." Mark guffawed.

Chaz stayed steadfast in his stern expression. Mark howled even louder, periodically gasping for breath.

# CHAPTER TWO

## Welcome...

An hour and wallet of cash later, Chaz arrived. The building was an old broom factory that had been converted into an apartment complex more than forty years ago; Dockside Lofts. Its mid-century metal sign with vintage incandescent light bulbs and rounded edges looked recently painted. The old brick building kept its large size. The grass surrounding the Loft's was clean cut. It looked as though someone had trimmed it a day or two prior. Trash was scattered about in the street and on the sidewalks with the focus of a teenager's notebook pages after their last day of class, but none of the debris reached the property.

Not even a single stray leaf from its dozens of trees lingered in the yard or parking lot. That impressed Chaz. All of the mowing, pruning, raking, and sweeping that had to be done for such a large property; he couldn't imagine doing so much yard work on a weekly basis. That was one of the benefits of moving into his house; it had no grass in the front or back to manage. Some leaves

9

would drift over from time to time, but that was easy to clean up. Ten dollars to a wandering teenager and the yard would be cleaned up in a matter of minutes. The other benefit was the neighborhood itself. He didn't have to worry about illegal activities, loitering, or even litter for that matter. It was a nice, quiet neighborhood with friendly and respectable neighbors.

Chaz's stomach twisted up in knots as he walked through the courtyard to the front door. "I can do this," he mumbled. "This is going to be great." He forced a smile to lighten his mood.

The double doors were ajar. He tried to look through their frosted windows, but he couldn't really make out anything. The doors led into a large vestibule with granite tiles and an umbrella rack. The transom window had the original building's name in gold leaf letters, Joey Cole & Company.

Pass the second set of double doors was the main hall. A thick dark blue and ivory rug covered some of the granite floor from the doorway to the back wall. Four square support pillars were evenly placed with small light fixtures on their sides. The walls were bare of any pictures or ornaments; only flat colors covered them. Everything looked clean, sterile, and expensive. He took caution with each step, trying not to ruin the building's purity.

To the right was the front desk. Its white speckled laminate had an ever so slight split at one of its edges, exposing dried glue underneath. He smiled, and relaxed knowing that if he did do any damage, he wouldn't be the one destroying the building's perfection. Chaz tapped twice on the silver call bell that sat on the counter.

He turned and leaned against the counter, waiting for a concierge or any other employee to show up and answer his questions. His fingertips glided over the counter's smooth surface as he examined the rest of the hall. Directly in front of him was a wooden gated freight elevator with a hanging 'out of service' sign. To the right was the staircase, stone with a thin rug down its center.

Chaz waited patiently for fifteen minutes before he decided to venture out on his own up the stairs. The sound of wood creaked from his weight on his first couple of steps. He stopped for a moment, looked down at the stairs, and then back at the hallway. He took the next step and heard nothing. Brushing it off, he scaled the rest of the flights in a mad dash to reach the fourth floor. He held onto the wooden railing to keep his balance. He stopped at the top of the stairs of his destination, taking a moment to calm his nerves, and to catch his breath. Chaz shook his arms to get rid of some of his jitters. The whole building was quiet.

"What am I going to say?" Chaz said to himself. He paced back and forth in the dimly lit hallway. Most of the lights were either muted or flickering. The light from the window above the stairs that could have helped brighten the area was covered with a thin layer of dust. His feet sank slightly on the plush carpet. It was like walking on a cloud. "Hey, Mr. Marvelous," Chaz mumbled, "I have a bunch of your action figures." He shook his head. "That's too aggressive. I need to keep it professional."

Chaz walked by three doors before reaching Mr. Marvelous' door, room 404. He reached out to knock. His hand stopped an inches from the door.

His phone rang; it was his wife. "Where are you?" Tracy asked.

"Oh, hey. I'm actually still at work. I have—"

"Work? You could have come up with a better excuse than that. Do you know what time it is?"

"I'm sorry. I should be home by eleven."

"Eleven? It's four in the morning right now." He checked his watch. 4:12. "I'm not doing this again."

She continued to talk but her voice faded from his conscious. The phone slipped from his hand and shattered on impact into three pieces; the front, the back, and the battery all bouncing in different directions.

"Come in," echoed through his head like his own internal monologue, but the voice was different. It was an uncomfortable feeling.

The door creaked open, breaking the seal between the hallway and Mr. Marvelous' domicile. The air that was held within smelled stale; as pungent as a nursing home. From what could be seen, the place was a mess. The term disarray couldn't encapsulate all of which was in front and surrounding him. Mr. Marvelous' room looked to be a shrine of his past glories. Newspaper articles were plastered on the walls like gold and platinum record plaques.

"Welcome," Mr. Marvelous said. He stood with his back blocking most of a large window. Its curtain raised all the way up. The full moon's light illuminated the room, casting its contents in a blue hue. He walked toward Chaz in a slow and calculated manner.

*Is this his secret lair? How long has he been living here? Why did he choose me?*

"Which one do you want me to answer first?" Mr. Marvelous asked. His voice was heavy and deep. His silhouette looked massive.

"What do you mean?" Chaz's voice quavered.

"How about why I chose you?"

"Uhh..."

"It's because you're a fan. You are a fan, aren't you?" Mr. Marvelous asked. His eyes pierced the shadows that cloaked the rest of his body. They loomed over Chaz, giving Mr. Marvelous a seemingly two foot height advantage. He had to physically look up to Mr. Marvelous like a child to a parent. Chaz stood fixated, ensnared by his gaze like the prey of a pulsating cuttlefish. "I've been watching you since you were a boy." After every couple of words Mr. Marvelous would pause for a moment. "I've been wanting to tell my story, and I want you to write it."

Chaz wiped his mouth, attempting to hide his smile. He was excited but he didn't want to show it. Then a thought rushed to the forefront; *I don't have any supplies with me. I'll just have to be honest with him.* "I rushed straight over here so I'm not really prepared for something like that."

"I had no plans of starting today. Honestly, I'm surprised you showed up at this hour." He paused for a moment. "This will be the first day of many. But you must promise two things."

"What's that?"

"Don't censor any of the stories. Everything I tell you is on the table. And two, don't tell anybody about our meetings until we have finished."

"How long will that take?"

"Two weeks. Several of hours a day, maybe less."

Chaz pretended to mull it over. "I can do that."

Mr. Marvelous' hand shot out into the light in front of Chaz. "Shake on it."

It was covered in a white and blue leather glove. Around his knuckles were a couple of brushed metal plates. Each one caught some of the light and reflected it right into Chaz's eyes. His eyes watered as he strained to not blink. He reached out and grabbed Mr. Marvelous' hand. The handshake was cold and firm.

Mr. Marvelous added in a quick squeeze at the end of it. The leather crackled as his grip tightened. "That's it."

"I really appreciate this," Chaz said. "I'm honored that you would choose me to write your story. There are so many other people that are probably far more capable than myself, but I will do my best."

"Your best is all I am asking for. This story can—no, it will—make your career and change your life. It can also help or hurt me depending on how you decide to tell the truth." Mr. Marvelous' eyes widened. "I trust you will respect my wishes."

Chaz's brow glistened with sweat. "Always."

"Good." Mr. Marvelous turned around and walked back toward the window. His silhouette covered Chaz's body in complete blackness. "It's late. You should go home. I will see you in two days."

Chaz nodded a couple of times. He opened his mouth to speak, but no words came out. What could he say? What should he say? He was just offered the job of a lifetime from his childhood hero. It could only go downhill from there, and saying the wrong thing would only accelerate the process.

# CHAPTER THREE

## The Switch

Chaz walked into the delicatessen and took off his jacket. "Welcome to Reed's," the workers shouted.

The place wasn't as crowded as normal at lunch. Construction on a nearby street had disrupted the free flow of pedestrian traffic on the deli's side of the block. There was a couple at the front paying their bill; several men in suits stood at the counter in line at the register. Most of them were wearing or holding orange construction helmets; and Mark, sitting on a stool at the opposite end of the counter. Chaz sat down beside him, placing his jacket on the empty stool beside himself.

"I thought you were off today," Chaz said. He picked up the laminated menu.

Mark nudged Chaz's arm with his elbow.

"Why do you have paint all over you?" Chaz checked his sleeve to make sure none of it brushed off on him.

Mark jabbed at his arm again.

"What?"

Mark discretely pointed in the direction of the cash register.

"Yeah, I think they are working on some building on the next block. Traffic is terrible out there."

"The lady," Mark murmured.

"Well she was mad, but I think I calmed her down."

"What are you talking about? Look at the lady in front of you." Mark pointed at her more aggressively.

"Oh." Chaz looked up and caught her eye. "Oh," he said, this time dragging out the word as he watched her. She smiled at him, and he smiled back. She was as beautiful as the waitress from the other day but more in their age range. They both stared at her with no reservation for discretion. "Is she new?" Chaz asked.

Mark shook his head. "I've never seen her before. I would've said something if I did."

"Looks like those guys beat you to it."

"They've been here for an hour now. Every time I try to have a conversation with her, they call her back over." Splotches of dried paint were all over Mark's hands and clothes.

"Maybe it's the paint. What's going on with all of the paint?" He poked at one of the patches on Mark's t-shirt.

"I was working on my kitchen before I left out," he said without removing his gaze.

"Did you eat like that?" He scrunched up his face, looking at the cupcake wrapper in front of Mark on the counter.

"I do it all of the time." Mark shrugged. "Never had a problem."

"I don't know why I am even looking at this menu; I'm not really hungry." Chaz turned toward Mark. "I saw Mr. Marvelous."

"Yeah."

"The first time I wasn't there for too long, but I got to shake his hand."

"Yeah."

"In fact, it was really dark in there, I couldn't see much. Nothing really happened that day, so that's why I didn't say anything until yesterday," Chaz said.

"Oh."

"You're not even paying attention."

"I think they're leaving, finally."

The men collectively got up from their seats and walked to the door. One straggled behind and handed the cashier his business card. She looked at the card for a couple of seconds, smirked, and then said, "I'll think about it," flicking the card between her finger tips. The confidence drained from the straggler's face as he turned and followed his colleagues out.

"Yes," Mark said with a smile, "shot down."

"How do you know?"

"I can see it on his face. I'm going to take advantage of that."

"Don't you think she is old enough to know about the 'savior' move? I don't think it's going to work."

"Every woman wants to be saved. That's what fairy tales are all about. Men swooping in to save them from some menacing group of ruffians."

"You're calling a group of white collar businessmen ruffians? Really?"

Mark laughed. "I was watching some old black and whites last night—it stuck. But it all makes sense though." He waived her over.

The woman brushed some hair out of her face as she approached. "Hey fellas. Do you need something?"

"No," Chaz said. "I'm good, thank you."

"I have a question..." Mark looked at her name tag. "Jessica." He sat up and leaned in closer to her. "I was having a friendly debate with my friend right here. The guy that gave you his card, was he hitting on you, or was he trying to sell you something?"

She gently bit her lower lip. "He asked me if I wanted to go out sometime."

"I knew it," Mark exclaimed. "Guys like that are always trying to flash their money."

"I know." She smiled. "I hate that. I mean it's not like I have the greatest job, but I'm not just looking for a guy with money."

"There's more to life than big money and cool cars, am I right?"

"Right," Jessica exclaimed.

Mark turned to Chaz and gave him a quick smile. "So, Jessica, I have been coming to this deli for years, but I don't remember ever seeing you here."

Chaz was half paying attention to Mark's words, with the other half on Jessica. He watched her mouth as she formulated every vowel and consonant. Her voice matched her body; strong and elegant with a hint of mystery. There was something there in the mix of her words and giggles that seemed oddly familiar. Every couple of words he heard it. His subconscious kept latching onto it as she spoke.

"Isn't that where your wife is from?" Mark asked.

"Yeah." Chaz dragged out the word. "What are we talking about?"

"We," Mark said while he gestured back and forth at Jessica and himself, "were talking about where she grew up. Are you all right over there? The paper has you working too hard."

"No." Chaz's brow furrowed. "I was daydreaming a little bit."

"You know," Mark said, "Chaz is working on an interview with—"

"I'm not supposed to talk about it," Chaz interjected.

"Don't worry, Jessica can keep a secret. Right?"

"Yeah, sure." She looked around, over both shoulders, and then leaned in close to them. She smelled of lavender. "Who is it," she whispered. The smell of cool mint drifted along with each word.

"I really can't."

"You were telling me about it the other day," Mark insisted.

"Please. I won't tell anyone. I cross my heart." She motioned the cross over her cleavage. Her two mounds looked as smooth as a freshly powered ski slope. Chaz and Mark both watched with raised eyebrows.

"Alright," Chaz said. Jessica beamed as she moved in even closer. "It's—"

The tiny bell at the entrance rang and the door slammed shut. Chaz looked up to see who came in. It was the old man from the other day, Frank. He was already halfway down the counter, making his way to his favorite seat by the time Chaz noticed. Chaz turned back around to speak to Jessica, but she was back at the cash register.

"Are you going to tell me what happened or are you just going to stare at her," Mark asked. Chaz turned to him. Mark was facing Chaz with his arms crossed. "Well?"

"Why did she leave? I was about to tell her."

"The waitress," Mark asked. "I tried to get you in on the conversation." Chaz looked back at her. She gave him a disgusted look and walked back to the kitchen. "She even tried to get your order a couple of times. You were just staring at her breasts."

"I thought she asked me about—"

"I hope you didn't mess that up for me. I was getting close to asking her out. I put in a lot of work for that."

Chaz looked over his shoulder toward Frank. Frank flashed a smile. Chaz twisted up his brow before turning back to Mark.


When I walked in, he was standing there. He looked exactly like my old action figure, standing in the same pose; his chest up and arms crossed, he stared out the window at The City. He wore the same blue and white themed suit. It was mostly white except for the band of blue that wrapped around his back and chest, forming an 'M' at his sternum.

"Welcome," he said. His voice resonated through my chest. I was like a little child in front of him, giddy and nervous at the same time. Before I could blurt out any admiration for him, he spoke again. "Please, have a seat." He gestured to his right.

In the center of his large living room were two chairs, placed across from each other, with a round coffee table in the middle. After I sat down, I looked around to really take notice of his place. Nothing seemed to match up with the outside of the building or the hallway. The place was massive. Its width looked like it took up the whole 4th floor, and the ceiling was at least two stories high. In the corner he had a small lamp for what looked like to be a study. The living room itself was lit purely by the sun. Three floor-to-ceiling windows allowed as much sunlight in as possible.

The size of the living room was made even more prominent from the lack of furniture. He had a simplistic, minimalist approach to his place. If he didn't need it, it wasn't there. For the most part, in the areas I could see, the place was very clean.

There was a pile of papers and books right beside the other chair. Some of them were daily newspapers. The pile was too far away for me to read any of the titles. Without even turning around, he said, "Don't jump ahead; you will ruin the story."

I was caught red-handed, but I still tried to play it off. "I was just trying to get comfortable in the chair."

He laughed at my attempt. "We will probably get along well. Before we start, how much do you know about me?"

"Everything."

He turned towards me. "Everything?"

Nothing changed about him. He looked exactly the same as he did fifty years ago; the square jaw, clear smooth skin, and his silver eyes. There were no wrinkles or crow's feet anywhere on his face, it was uncanny. "Well not everything, but I've read everything I could get my hands on."

"Then he smiled at me. The whole thing felt really awkward."

"What do you mean?" Mark asked.

"Well, the first part of the smile, the part with his mouth closed, that seemed natural. Next, came a slow teeth reveal over few seconds." Chaz mimicked the smile as he explained it.

"All right, I get it." Mark looked visibly disturbed. "You can stop now."

After that creepy smile, he walked over. "Where do you want to start?"

"Oh," I said while digging through my jacket's pockets. "Give me one second." I checked each pocket twice, before I started to panic. I remember thinking, did I leave my Dictaphone at the office? "Just one more second. I know I have it on me somewhere." I patted myself down a few times, and still I came up empty. I looked at him with regret. I was right on the precipice of apologizing for my lack of professionalism and then he did that smile again.

Chaz mimicked the smile again for Mark.

"Stop. I'm not going to be able to sleep tonight."

They both cracked up.


Mr. Marvelous pointed at the table. "Your recorder is right there."


"You must have put it down as soon as you sat down," Mark said.

"I was thinking the same thing."


I pressed the record button. "So, since some of the readers might not know who you are, where you're from, or how your legend began, let's start from the beginning."

"Beginnings—are always so boring," he said, "but you're interviewing me and not the other way around." Mr. Marvelous sat down in the chair across from me, crossed his legs at the ankle. His boots had exposed metal plate at each toe box. Their blue shoestrings hung loosely at the sides. "Most people thought I was some sort of alien from outer space who narrowly escaped a dying planet by way of an escape pod when I was a child. That's all rubbish." He reached over, slid some of the papers to the side, knocking them to the floor. He picked up a thick leather bound photo album and handed it to me. The cover had a picture of him as an infant. He was a chubby faced, pale baby. Well...he might have been pale. I can't really be too sure since it was a black and white photo.


"How do you know it was him," Mark asked.

"Who else would it be?"

"Could have been one of those placeholders. You know, the pictures that are in frames when they're still at the store."

"Shut up. Anyway..."

He looked like a regular child, maybe a little tall for his age, but that's about it. Every picture after that showed the same, nothing out of the ordinary. As I flipped through the pages, he continued to talk.

"I was raised the same way as everyone else. I played with toys; I ran around and jumped in puddles; I climbed trees; I laughed, cried, and played catch like all of my friends. I was like everyone else at the time."

"Are any of those friends still around? Have you talked to them?"

"I don't know." He looked away. "I didn't keep in touch with them once I moved."

I got the impression that either something might have happened or it was too early to ask questions like that. So I steered him back to the question about his powers. "So you were just like all of the other kids growing up?"

"Yes." He turned his attention back on me. "I don't know why I was born with powers. No one else in my family could do any of these things. And it's not like I was in some kind of strange car accident involving steel drums of radiation."

Mark's eyebrow raised. "Really," Mark muttered.

"Where were you raised?"

"Two miles outside of The City, in Grover's Field." He used his thumb to point behind him. "It's a nice, quiet area."

"I know the area," Chaz said. "My parents were thinking about moving me out there when I was going to middle school. They said the schools were better there."

"It all depends on the teacher and how you learn."

"I agree." I nodded. "Luckily for me, my parents decided not to make the move. I think it had something to do with financial issues."

"I'm sure you didn't understand at the time."

"Not at all. I was just glad to stay in my neighborhood and be with my friends." I chuckled.

"The simple life of a child, totally oblivious to the financial responsibilities of the adults that rule their lives. To be young again; one can only dream."

"Yeah." I gestured at him. "You still have your youthful looks and a spring in your step. How old are you?"

"You wouldn't believe me if I told you."

"You're Mr. Marvelous, why wouldn't I believe you?"

"Maybe not you," he said, "but what about your audience?" He smiled that same smile. This time more brief than the last. His eyes narrowed. "I'll leave it up to you to figure it out."

"If I guess right, would you tell me?"

He said nothing and continued to stare at me, and then came that smile. Each time he did it, it made me more uncomfortable, so I changed the question. "When did you first realize that you had these super human abilities?"

"I was about sixteen." He reached over to assist me in flipping the pages to get to the right time period. There, in the very middle of the album were two pictures, both on opposite pages. He pointed at the pictures. "This is before," pointing at the picture on the left, "and two days after." Both pictures were basically the same. He was standing by himself in the middle of a yard or field of some kind. I didn't see a house or anything. It might have been his family's, but I don't know. He was just standing there, arms by his side, looking at whoever was holding the camera. It's still hard to imagine that that skinny, bashful looking kid, grew up to be Mr. Marvelous.

"Do you see it yet?" He asked.

"See what?" I asked right before noticing. It was the tiniest thing. You would have to really focus to notice but it was there. Once I saw it, it was clear as day."

"What was it?" Mark asked.

"It's hard to explain."

"What do you mean? Was it some kind of scar or a new hair cut?"

Chaz shook his head.

"Did he look bigger or something? Did he look a little stronger?"

Chaz paused for a minute. He looked up at the ceiling. His eyes darted back and forth. "I don't know." He shook his head again. "You would have to have seen it."

"Well then how do you know the pictures were different?"

"Because... I could see the change. Just trust me." Chaz continued with the story.

"Two days before the picture on the right, I was with a group of friends. We were doing what we normally would, talking about things that happened in school. Right before it happened, we ran out of things to talk about. Then," He said, leaning forward in the chair. "My vision shifted, ever so slightly, before the old world started dripping down around me. Everything became brighter and more saturated. It was like I landed in Oz. Everything changed." He rubbed the chair's arm rests. "Nothing looked or felt the same anymore. I was stronger, faster, and my vision was clearer."

"Just like that?" I said, excited by the whole idea of his power seemingly coming out of nowhere. He was born with a purpose. "Like a flip of a switch?"

"Exactly."

"How did you feel that night?"

"Confused," he said. "I was confused about my change in sight. Nothing else was different yet."

"Did you talk to anyone about it?"

"No, not at all. I didn't think it was a big deal. I wasn't in pain or lacking one of my senses; there is only that slight shift in my perception—and I thought—it will pass and everything will be back to normal when I wake up in the morning. That didn't happen."

"Was it gradual? The process, I mean."

He nodded. "If you consider a week enough." He uncrossed his legs, sliding himself closer to the edge of the chair.

"I don't know if I could have done that," Chaz remarked. "Being that young and developing super strength and speed, I don't think I could have kept that secret. I would have at least told you."

"You damn right. We could have been a dynamic duo." Mark laughed. "I wouldn't wear the underwear and tights though."

"How else is the citizens going to know you're the sidekick?"

"Sidekick? We're the same age. I don't think it works that way."

"You act like it's a real job. There's no set rules for a sidekick." Chaz's brow furrowed. "Right?" He rubbed his forehead as he thought, massaging out the wrinkles. "There had to be, right? At least one hero with sidekick around the same age."

Mark shook his head. "Besides, being a sidekick is like being an apprentice. You can't teach anything if you're still learning yourself. Plus—can you picture a grown man following another grown man around, swinging from roof to roof with color coordinated underwear and stockings. That's something you can only convince a child to wear."

Chaz grinned. "He said sixteen. So neither one of us would be grown at the time. We could have pulled it off."

"Who are you telling?" Mark thumped on his chest. "I've been grown since fifth grade."

"Ah, shut it up."


I nodded as I thought about his answer. "What's your real name?" He looked at me like he was shocked by my question. I know it's his secret identity and all, but it's not like he's still an active hero. "I can keep that out of the article if you like." I hoped that would give him some confidence in me.

"Let's leave that for the last day. You'll always have that to look forward to."


"You don't already know it?"

"No. There was never any mention of it. He's always kept that part of himself secret."

"It's probably one of those superhero names like Thaddeus Turner or Matias Morgan."

Chaz scrunched up his face.

"Yeah, you're right. That's too cliché. It's probably more simple than that." Mark nodded his head and brushed through his hair. "Yeah... it's got to be a name that fits in with the times." He snapped his finger and then tapped several times on the counter. "How about Charlie? Dean? Gene? Fred? Or maybe—"

An arm reached over grabbing the ketchup that sat in front of Chaz. He leaned back to avoid any mistaken contact. The waiter handed the bottle over to Frank. "Here you go. Do you need anything else?" Frank smiled and shook his head to the question.

Chaz watched as Frank poured the ketchup on top of his sunny side up eggs and hash browns. "Are you just rattling off old actors?" He turned back to Mark.

"Yeah. What's wrong with that?"

This time, I could feel Mr. Marvelous' smile was coming, so I changed the subject. "How long was it before you stopped your first crime?" It worked like a charm. I stopped him right at the beginning.

He looked at me for a few seconds. It was intense, like when we would have the stare down with my cat, Bamboo, to see who would break eye contact first. He looked away before getting up from the chair, crowning me the victor, but just like with Bamboo, I still felt like I had lost. He walked back over to the windows and looked out over The City. "We will save that for our next meeting."

I cleared my throat. "All right." I stood up and slowly walked over to the door. I wanted to shake his hand, but he had a 'hurry up and get out' type of vibe going on, so that's what I did.

"Wow. He didn't even see you out?"

"Nope. If it was someone else, I might have said something, but he is not the kind of person you want to piss off."

"Yeah," Mark said. "That makes sense."

"After that," Chaz's left eye twitched, "I remember standing in front of his door, my arm out stretched preparing to knock, and not being sure of what to say."

"Why were you about to knock?"

Chaz continued with his story.

I had the oddest feeling of déjà vu, and then my phone rang. I didn't bother with looking at the caller ID. "Hello."

"Where are you?" I've been worried sick."

"Hi, honey. I'm on the other side of The City. I'm about to meet Mr. Marvelous."

"Who?"

"You know, Mr. Marvelous."

"Who is that?"

I couldn't believe she didn't know who he was. "He used to be a hero."

"Wait a minute, you're out with that pervert?"

"I'm just here to interview him. That's it."

"Right."

"I'll be home by eleven."

"Eleven," she shouted. "It's 4 in the morning."

Four in the morning? I thought to myself. I checked my watch to make sure, 4:12. I looked around the hallway as if I was going to find the abundance lost time somewhere lurking in the shadows.

She continued, "You've been gone all night, hanging around with your perverted, wino, hero friend, and now you're telling me you're still not on your way back? You said you were going to change. You either make your way back here in thirty minutes or our marriage is over. I mean it this time."

"Don't do that. I'm on my way, right now. I love you."

# CHAPTER FOUR

## Early Career

Chaz and Mark walked into Reed's together. The bell above the door rang as loud as ever. The place was crowded for a weeknight. Customers lined the walls near the door waiting for their party's name to be called. On an ordinary day, the house rules would be to seat yourself, but today, they would have to wait for a table like everyone else.

Mark approached the hostess, a tall woman; two inches shorter than him. She wore a standard black and white uniform; her name tag pinned to her shirt. "Hello—," Mark said as he glanced down, "Mercy."

"Hello, sir. How many?"

"Just two. How long is the wait?"

Mercy looked at the paper on the hostess stand. She scanned over it for a couple of seconds and then looked around at the other guests standing and sitting by the door, "thirty minutes."

"Alright. My name is Mark."

She wrote down his name. "I will let you know when your table is ready."

"Thank you. We'll be waiting outside."

Mark and Chaz slipped past a group of patrons on their way through the door. The air was warm for the season. Brown leaves crunched under their feet as the two walked to the corner of the block. The streets were busy with rush hour traffic. Chaz stopped at the light pole, leaning against it with his shoulder. Mark rested his crossed arms on the top of the newspaper vending machine that was beside it. The smells from the deli wafted through the evening breeze.

"I'm starving," Mark said. "I've been so busy today. I didn't get to eat lunch." He looks up to Chaz. "We should go to a convenience store. I need a snack or something."

"The closest one is five blocks away. I'm not walking five blocks in these shoes." Chaz had on a pair of stiff leather soled dress shoes. They shined in the lamp post's spotlight. "They haven't been broken in yet."

"We can drive there."

"And lose my parking spot?" Chaz shook his head. "You'll be fine. It's only a half hour wait." Chaz reached into his suit jacket pocket and pulled out a mint. "Do you want one?"

"No," Mark said, deflated. "That will just make things worse."

Chaz shrugged and ate the mint. The wrapper dropped out of his hand as he leaned back on to the pole. Mark watched as it fell to the ground beside Chaz's shoes.

Mark walked over, picked up the tumbling wrapper, and placed it in the nearby trash can. "Why don't you wear loafers with rubber soles? They're comfortable. You can walk for days in those."

"Look at me—I'm wearing a three piece suit." He stood up and spun around, showing off his outfit; spreading his jacket to expose his matching vest and starched shirt. "This isn't some cheap bargain bin suit."

Mark walked back over to the vending machine and hopped on top of it, unimpressed by Chaz's outfit. "You can hardly move around in the thing."

"You don't match up a suit like this," he waved his hands down his outfit, "with a pair of string-less loafers, let alone rubber soles. This is how professionals dress. I'm not lounging in the house with a smoking jacket."

"Fashion over comfort. You can't get any real work done in something like that. You don't even want to walk a couple of blocks."

"I just came from working." Chaz checked his watch. Its gold trim shined under the streetlight. They still had more than twenty minutes left. "A man's attire is a testament of his life. If you pay attention to your wardrobe, you will pay attention to the rest of your life. My grandfather told me that when I was young. No loafers for me."

"Humph." Mark shifted his body to face Chaz. He looked down at his old dusty trainers. "Do you know what I learned? Hard work shows through your clothes, and you should always respect a hard worker. They're the ones that make the world go round." He hopped off of the newspaper vending machine. "Do you know the difference between guys like that—" Mark pointed at Chaz's shoes, "and guys like this?" He then pointed at his own shoes.

Chaz slipped his hands into his pants pockets. He raised his eye brows and shrugged. "Tell me."

"Rubber soles do the work, travel the miles, get dirty, and keep their traction when things get slippery. Leather soles have a hard time keeping their footing when the weather gets rough, they'd rather get carried than make it off of their own sweat, and when it's time to work they tell someone else to do it."

"Excuse me," a man said as he and his date passed by, their arms wrapped together. Mark stepped aside to let them pass. Chaz watched as the man guided his date across the street.

"Is that how you see me?" Chaz asked.

"No. I know you," Mark said. "I grew up with you. But I can see that you're flirting with it."

Chaz caught a glimpse of himself in the deli's window, his face obscured by its handwritten sign; Reed's Delicatessen, open since 1913. He stared at his shoes.

"I was out of line." Mark walked over and placed his hand on Chaz's shoulder. "Sorry about that. I'm just really hungry." Mark took back his hand. "I'll go to the store by myself. The table should be ready by the time I get back." He crossed the street at the crosswalk without another word, an anxious pep in his step.

Chaz continued to stare at the window. "I'm not like that. Am I?" He said, unsettled by the allegation.

"Excuse me young man."

Chaz turned to find the voice. It was Frank, waddling his way down the sidewalk towards him.

"I don't want to cut myself," he said with a smile. His face crinkled from the motion.

Chaz stepped out of the way, avoiding the pole in the process. "Huh?"

"Looking sharp."

Chaz gave a light nod. "Thank you, sir."

"Call me Frank." He reached his hand out.

"Frank." Chaz shook his hand. It was a strong, firm grip. "Chaz."

"Pleased to meet you Chaz." He looked down at Chaz's shoes. "They look like mirrors. You would have done well in the military."

"Funny that you would say that, I learned how to polish my shoes from my grandfather. He was in the navy."

Frank stood erect. "Where I lay my anchor is my home."

"You were in the service?"

"No. I've had my battles but never on the open sea. I was never much of a swimmer." He slumped back down to his normal posture. "I was a—beat cop."

"Keeping the people safe is commendable no matter how you do it."

"Thank you." Frank grabbed his hand again and shook it. "Maybe you will inspire others to feel that way."

"You're very welcome." Chaz patted him on his shoulder. He didn't feel frail like he expected. "Let me get the door for you."

Chaz escorted Frank inside of Reed's. The deli still looked the same. People lined the wall near the door, waiting for their chance to sit and eat. He thought about asking for an update from the hostess, but he didn't want to bother her. She looked busy with the other patrons vying for her attention. He walked back outside into the cool air. A couple minutes later Mark strolled over.

"Did they call us yet?" Mark asked.

"No, but we should be next. It's been about forty minutes now."

"I'm not trying to sit out here all night." Mark went inside and straight to the hostess. "Hi. How much time is left on our table?"

"It's ready. The table is being cleaned off."

"Which one?" Mark peeped around her to see all of the tables. "That one right there?" A young man removed the dishes from the tabled and placed them into a bin.

The hostess turned around to see which one he was talking about. "Yes. He has to wipe it down."

"We have been standing up for a while outside," Mark pointed at Chaz, "and his feet hurt. We are going to sit down at the table while he finishes." He tapped Chaz on the arm. "Come on."

They walked over to the booth and sat down. The bus boy finished up wiping down the table and made his way to the back. Chaz waved his menu back and forth over the table. "What did you get at the store?"

"I bought a candy bar."

"I think I'm going to get a milkshake."

"So what happened with Mr. Marvelous?"

"Right." Chaz placed down the menu.

I heard him say, "Welcome," as I opened the door to his place. His place was brighter than before. He stood at the window overlooking The City.

"Have a seat," he said and gestured to his right. He was still wearing his costume from the other day. It looked as clean as the first day that I saw him. I walked into the room and sat down in the chair.

Chaz's brow furrowed. "Everything looked the same but sort of opposite."

"What do you mean," Mark asked.

"Instead of the study being to the left, it was on the right side where the chair and table was. The bedroom was now on the opposite side."

"Were they the same chairs and everything?"

Chaz rubbed the top of his head in a circular motion. "Yeah."

"You probably mixed things up."

"You're probably right," Chaz pondered. "I was thinking the same thing."

The stack of papers and the photo album still sat on the side of the chair.

"Where do you want to start," Mr. Marvelous asked.

"How about your abilities?"

"My abilities?"

"Some of the readers might know," I said, "but just in case, could you tell me what they are?"

He nodded, most of his attention was still on The City. "I have superhuman strength, speed, durability, endurance, reflexes, vision, and—I can fly, but my ground speed is quicker."

"Thank you."


"Thank you?" Mark questioned.

"I don't know why I said it," Chaz shrugged. "I was still nervous and excited."


"Can you tell me about your early career?"

He turned towards me and stared for a bit. "Sure." He walked over to his chair, picked up the photo album, opened it to the first page, and handed it to me. "It was a year after I felt the change." He smiled at me, but this time it was different. He didn't have that last part at the end. It was warm and looked more genuine. "From there I decided to fight crime full-time. I waited to move out on my own first. That way I wouldn't have to worry about something happening to my parents or them snooping through my things. I needed my own proverbial fortress of solitude. Once I got that, I needed a costume and name."


"What is going on with all of the superman references?" Mark asked.

"I think it was because all of his powers are so similar," Chaz said.

"I know, but superman isn't even real, and he is. People don't compare their lives to Pan just because they can play the flute."

"So what? It's just a simile."

"You mean a metaphor."

"Same thing."

"Nope," Mark insisted, "but—I see what you are saying. For whatever reason though, it's rubbing me the wrong way."


"How did you come up with your name?"

"Flip to the fourth page," Mr. Marvelous said as he walked over to his study. On the fourth page, there were two sheets of lined paper. Their edges were yellowed from time. Each paper was covered with different names: Speeder, Titan, Crusher, Him, etc. All of them in some way tried to convey his abilities or make him stand out somehow. Out of all those potential names he had but one circled.


"Mr. Marvelous?" Mark asked.

"You would think so, but no, it was a different name."

"What was it then?

"Kid Power."

"Really? Kid Power?" Mark laughed.

"I know, I know. Let me finish."

While he was in the other room, he said something to me, but I couldn't hear him. "Mr. Marvelous," he repeated. "The name sounded fantastic and prestigious at the same time." He walked back out with his first costume in hand. I became ecstatic. I leaped out of my seat and rushed to meet him halfway. Right before I could touch it, he moved it away. I looked up at him, questioning his change in heart. He towered over me. I knew he was a couple of inches taller before the first interview, but the reality of it was on a totally different plane. My head was almost completely arched back by the time I could see his face.

"It is very old and one of a kind," Mr. Marvelous said.

I understood. It's a relic of one of Earth's biggest icons. It could have fallen apart if I would have handled it too rough.

"He's acting just like you with that damn letter," Mark muttered.

I nodded my head to show that I understood. He unfolded the suit and held it close to his body like he was testing it out in a department store. I stared at the garment intently. Inspecting everything from its blue/white palette to its sloppy stitching and mismatched fabrics. I had to fight the urge to rub the material between my fingers. The suit looked bulky, like it would have been a sauna in the summer. It even still had sweat stains around the arm pit. Surprisingly, it didn't smell though. In fact, I didn't smell anything at all.

"I wore that suit for about six months before I became popular. After that people were offering to recreate it. They even had a contest."

"That's cool of them to do that." Mark's eyebrows raised. "You know, you could almost take that as an insult." He flashed a smile.

"Insult?"

Mark nodded.

Chaz laughed. "Because his original suit looked so bad, huh? That's funny."

"I think I remember hearing about that. It was in the papers right?"

"Yes. It was open to any one that wanted to participate." He stopped for a moment and narrowed his eyes. "Do you know who won the competition?"

"I should know this. Give me a second." I already knew the answer, but like I said before, I didn't want to seem too much like a geek, so I pretended to think it over. "It was some clothing company right? Richard & Dudley."

"R & D." He smiled. "After they won, I wore the suit that they created. They also wanted me to endorse them, so I did." He shrugged. "I really needed the money. I think they could tell by the way my other suit looked." Mr. Marvelous chuckled. "The suit I am wearing right now is the..."

"Mach 3 marvel."

He nodded with a wink. I smiled from ear to ear. He then gestured to my seat. I don't think he wanted to continue with me up-under him for the rest of the day. By the time I sat down, he had already put the uniform back and was sitting across from me.

Mr. Marvelous' hands clutched the front of his armrests. "The initial crimes I stopped were all small time: breaking and entering, stolen pocketbooks, and such. All of them were easy to stop. The problem was the fact that I wasn't good at controlling myself." He scratched his ear. "I was putting a lot of people in the hospital."

"How serious were the injuries?"

"The cops were looking for a serial assaulter."

"A serial assaulter? Is that even a thing?" Mark asked.

Chaz shook his head with a shrug. "I don't think he even knew," he said. "He just looked out the windows, studied the landscape, and kept on talking."

"I—started to train on my off days. One of the things I would do involved gently squeezing eggs to help control my strength. I also did some other things to make everything more manageable." He nodded. "I spent a lot of time on my speed and flight as well."

"I understand." I nodded. "Because even if you dial your strength back, you could still hurt them if you were moving too fast."

"Right." I think I impressed him. He turned around to face me and became more lively. "After training myself for a while, there were more positive remarks about me in the paper."

"What would you call 'a while'?"

"Three weeks." He emphasized the number by holding up his last three fingers. "More or less, three weeks." He tucked his lips. "After that, I got my name from a young woman. I saved her from being assaulted. While she was being interviewed, the patrolman asked what she thought of her savior, and she called me marvelous." Mr. Marvelous grinned, baring most of his teeth. They glistened in the light.

"Oh," Mark interjected. "I was about to bring up the fact that he never really answered that question."

"That's why you have to listen to the full story first."

"Sometimes you leave things out."

"Like what?"

"I don't know," Mark shrugged, "That's why I asked."

Chaz gave a stern look with a hard exhale.

"Alright. Finish the story."

So I asked him, "Is that around the time you started to get endorsements?"

He looked at me for a moment, locking his eyes with mine. "So many endorsements, you wouldn't believe." He flipped the photo album I had in my lap to the first page. It was pictures of him with a bunch of wealthy people.

"How do you know they were wealthy?"

"He told me. And because the way they were dressed."

Everybody in the picture was dressed in a tux or a ball gown except for him. He decided to stick with his crime fighting uniform. They were in some hall that used to be downtown. He said it was a really popular place when he was young, but they demolished it twenty years later; it was a part of the downtown revitalization project.

"I had made millions throughout the years. If they didn't pay with money, I would get paid in other ways; free products, housing and food. As long as I kept saving The City, they kept giving me things."

"So you received free things for saving people from assault, robbery, and the occasional cat in the tree." I made sure to put "occasional cat in the tree" in air quotes to avoid having him feel insulted.

"No. That was also around the time the villain and, a couple of years later, the super villains were born. After a while, something would come along and balance things out. The whole thing makes sense now—decades later. You can't have light without the darkness." He threw his hands up and leaned back in the chair. "And so they came, through the cracks and crevices. They came from all around, looking to tear down what I had built up."

"Which one was the first?"

"Dr. Charge and Positron."

"The mad scientist...?"

He nodded. "Dr. Charge was one of those insane scientist types. He felt as though I was ruining The City. He believed that one person shouldn't have as much power as I did. Positron was the

46

robot he created to help him defeat me. It was a primitive looking thing. It looked like a trash can on tank tracks."

Mark laughed. It was initially a small chuckle but it snowballed into a real 'knee slapper'.

"What's so funny?"

Mark struggled to get the words out. "He was battling a robot from Mystery Science Theater 3000. It probably had pipe cleaner eyebrows."

Chaz fought the urge to laugh. It was a battle he almost lost. He had Mark's infectious laugh and the joke itself to fight off to continue the story.

"I don't know if the possibility of me underestimating him was his 'Ace in the hole', but I fell right into it," Mr. Marvelous explained. "That robot must have zapped me fifteen times with its electro gun before I dismantled it. Then, one quick chop to Dr. Charge and he was unconscious."

"He showed me the chop," Chaz added.

"How did it look?" Mark asked.

"It was nothing impressive, but I'm sure with his strength it would do some damage."

"Were you hurt from the electro gun?"

"Not really." He shook his head. "The pain was equivalent to a light static shock. After that, The City held a small parade in my honor. There were several floats and a college marching band. It was a great time, but better times were on the way. There was a period of civil rest, but then," Mr. Marvelous shrugged, "a couple of months later, I was back to fighting crime. The next villain, Dynamo, was more powerful."

"I've never heard of Dynamo."

"Really?" He smiled, baring his teeth. "I thought you knew everything." Mr. Marvelous continued before I could respond. "She was really tough."

"Dynamo was a woman?"

He nodded his head. "That's what made it so difficult. I couldn't beat her up like a normal guy; she was a woman after all. Though, she did pack a mean wallop."

"Where did she come from? What did she look like? How many times did you fight her?" I leaned forward.


"Switched back to a fan again, huh?" Mark said.

"Yeah. He noticed too."


"One question at a time. Turn to the middle of the book."

I opened the album to the right page on the first try. There was a picture of her on one side and information about her on the other. It looked kind of like a trading card. It had her real name and everything.

"Well," Mark said.

Chaz shook his head. "Uh-uh. I can't tell you that."

"Why not?"

"From what he told me, she's moved on with her life, and I don't want to throw a wrench into that."

"I want to see what she looks like. I'm not going to hunt her down or show up at her house. Have you looked her up yet?"

"I looked, but I haven't found much. All I found were two blurry pictures and neither one was without her costume."

"I could find some for you."

"No."

"I'm an expert with search engines."

"No," Chaz repeated.

"Come on. It could help you with the story," Mark said. "Do you remember the time I found Kiesha for you?"

"Who?" Chaz's brow furrowed.

"The girl we met at the amusement park. She was checking you out the whole time." The memory still wasn't clicking for Chaz. "You were too scared to talk to her," Mark added, "so I got her name for you."

Chaz nodded. "I remember now. I ran up on their bus but when I saw her I just turned right back around." Chaz smiled and shook his head.

"All I had was her name and the school bus's plates. I found her, her school, and her email address in a couple of days." Mark counted each finding on his fingers.

"And?" Chaz retorted.

"And—I could do the same for Dynamo, but for her pictures."

"I know you. You're not going to stop with her pictures."

"You're always trying to hide girls from me."

"Alright. How about I describe her costume?"

Mark grinned.

"She wore baggy blue overalls, yellow construction boots, black finger-less gloves, and a tight white tank top. I think she wore a hat too."

Mark's eyebrows dropped. "Well, that was disappointing."

"It wasn't the most creative costume, but she didn't look bad in it."

"What about her face?"

"I couldn't see her face. He had it marked out with a sharpie or something like that. I do know she was white with blonde hair and really tall."

"How tall?"

"Six-foot-three."

"What about the pictures you saw when you did the search?"

"Both of them had her face covered."

Mark sucked his teeth. "What are the odds on that?"

"In the first one, she was stretched out on the ground, and Mr. Marvelous was standing over her unconscious body. It must have been taken by some amateur photographer. There was debris from the fight everywhere, and some of it was in between her face and the camera lens. The other one was after she was arrested. They put a black bag over her head for transport."

"It has to be another one somewhere," Mark said.

"I fought her twice in my career. The first time was out of nowhere. She snuck up behind me while I was helping with a truck accident. The first hit made me stumble. The second sent me flying through Lover's Fountain.

"Lover's Fountain?"

"Yes. There was a fountain that used to be in The Square."

"There was a fountain in The Square?"

"Ages ago. They replaced it, but it got destroyed for the second and final time three years later."

"Would you say she was about as strong as you or stronger?"

"Let's say, I broke a sweat dueling with her that day." Mr. Marvelous walked back over to the window. The sun slowly tucked itself in behind the clouds that began to blanket the sky. "Most of the fights I've been in were undemanding," Mr. Marvelous said, staring out at the transitioning sky. "No one really knew the extent of my abilities so it was easy to fake an injury or two. So sometimes, not often mind you," he nodded, "I would take a punch on the chin or get knocked through a building." He turned around to look at me; his hands behind his back. "Only empty buildings, of course."

Mark's upper lip started to quiver.

"It's all showmanship." Mr. Marvelous paced back and forth as he continued. "Nobody wants to see a boxer knock out every opponent in the first 10 seconds. No." He shook his head. "They want to enjoy it; a battle of the ages. They want to see something that will make them rush home at the end of the day and tell their family about it." He smiled. His back was towards me, but I could hear it in his voice. "So that's what I gave them. Winning those fights was easy and inevitable. They would get me some cheers, but the real admiration came from the struggle. When the people thought you were suffering or hurt, they were more excited. And when you battled back and won, it was like being in the Colosseum." He stopped in place and turned to me. His eyes twinkled like stars. "Underdogs always get the most love," he said, slowly nodding. "Everyone loves an underdog."

Mark looked around the room smoldering.

"What? Something happened?"

Mark shook his head a couple of times.

"What's wrong?" Chaz asked.

"Nothing." Mark turned back to Chaz. He tucked his lips with a heavy exhale. "What else happened?"

Chaz was perturbed. "Well, after that he told me about how his life changed."

Mark's jaw muscles flexed as he waited for Chaz to continue.

"Maybe I should just save it for the next time."

"Yeah." Mark got up as soon as the words left his mouth and walked out of the door.

# CHAPTER FIVE

## French Maid

"You are not going to believe this," Chaz said as Mark approached the booth.

"Hold up. Let me get something first." Mark walked over to the deli's counter and spoke to the nearby waitress. She walked to the kitchen and came back with a large cornbread muffin. He handed her some cash and unwrapped the muffin as he walked over to Chaz. "What happen to you the other day?"

"What do you mean?"

"I was in here for a couple of hours waiting for you," Mark said.

"Wednesday?"

"Yeah. You never answered your phone either."

"I was in here—with you—Wednesday." Chaz retracted his head a little. "You're working too hard."

"Last time I saw you, it was Monday." Mark ripped the muffin in half and placed both halves on the bread plate. He buttered both sides as he continued to talk. "The story was about his early career and him getting beat up by a vacuum cleaner."

"Ha Ha," Chaz mocked with a straight face. "It wasn't a vacuum cleaner, and that was Wednesday." Chaz reached down to his pocket. "Look at this. I make sure to keep everything on my calendar." He pulled out his phone and handed it over to Mark. "And so you don't have any other excuses, I'm not even going to open it."

Mark turned the phone's screen on. "What's the pin? Your old address?"

Chaz sucked his teeth. "I need a new pin."

"See. The very first thing that came up." Mark showed Chaz the phone.

"Ten missed calls?" Chaz said to himself. All of the calls were from Wednesday. His brow twisted up.

"I told you."

"I thought I was here." Chaz checked the time for each of the calls. "What..."

Frank bumped into their table on his way to his favorite seat. The jolt stopped Chaz in the middle of his sentence; his mouth still partially open. His mind reached for his last thought, but instead it was caught by Frank's presence. Chaz watched as Frank passed by.

"He didn't even apologize. It's like manners don't apply just because you're old," Mark said. He stuffed one half of the muffin into his mouth. A waitress followed close behind Frank as he waddled by at a snail's pace. She stopped at their table and waited until Frank moved out of ear shot.

"He is always running into people. I can't stand him," she declared.

"Don't be so hard on him. He's having a hard enough time as it is," Chaz said. His eyes were still locked on Frank's movements. He watched him struggle to sit down comfortably on the corner stool. After Frank got situated, he looked up and locked eyes with Chaz. He gave a courtesy wave as if he knew what Chaz had said. Chaz nodded and turned back to the table. "He didn't mean anything by it."

"You two supposed to be friends now? You know he wasn't waving at you. He was calling over the cashier," Mark said. Chaz looked back and saw the cashier at the end of the counter talking to Frank. The waitress and Mark laughed. "Like I said, he doesn't care."

The waitress popped her gum a couple of times before she spoke. "Jessica isn't on the schedule for today."

"She told me she was working this week," Mark said, "Do you have her number?"

Her head jerked back. "I can't give you that." She stood up and pulled a notepad and pencil out of her apron. "How am I supposed to know if you really know her or not? You could be some kind of creep," she said with a snarky expression.

"Creep? Really?" Mark said.

She popped her gum once more. "I've got tables." The waitress walked off to take a patron's order.

Chaz and Mark looked at each other for a moment. Mark was the first to break the silence. "So it's not exclusively old farts that have problems with their manners," Mark said. His upper lip started to curl up. "I just wanted to know—what was going on with Jessica, and then the next thing I know, I get labeled a creep."

"Speaking of Jessica—listen to this."

"Alright." Mark picked up the last half of his muffin and took a huge bite.


"Welcome," Mr. Marvelous said as I opened the door to his place.

Two newly placed square pillars were on opposite sides of the apartment. His room and the study had some new sliding doors. To my left, closer to the bedroom, was a long wooden table with three or four chairs and several plastic bags on it. They looked like they could have been grocery bags or something.

"Have a seat." He gestured to his right.

My attention went back to Mr. Marvelous. He was in his normal position, standing in front of the windows, his hands behind his back. "What's going on with the—" I must've forgotten about the raised floor near the door, because I missed the step and stumbled. I managed to get my footing before I tumbled to the ground. When I looked up, he was looking right at me.


"He didn't say anything?"

"Nope," Chaz said while shaking his head. "It was like nothing even happened." Chaz raised his eyebrows. "I don't think I would have wanted him to say anything. I was already embarrassed."

I walked to the chair and sat down. It was one of those office chairs with wheels and thin padding. Most of the windows were open, allowing the cool breezes to circulate throughout the room. Each gust swept the linen curtains up into the air and poured the smell of the bay's water into the room. I tilted my head back as I soaked in the smells.

"The smell reminded me of the time we were on that class trip to Midfield Beach and I had the bright idea to get buried up to my neck in sand." Chaz smiled.

Mark laughed. "And the beach had all those sand crabs."

"I looked like I had chicken pox from all of the pinching."

"I remember your mother kept inviting kids over so you could pass it along." Mark continued to laugh.

"You know, I just found out about pox parties when I was in college." Chaz chuckled. "Must have been disappointing when they found out I wasn't sick." Chaz continued to laugh to himself. "I still hate crabs."

"Where do you want to start?" Mr. Marvelous asked.

"Success." I adjusted myself and the seat height. The chair was really stiff compared to the other ones. I wasn't slouching as much because of the support, but sitting up so erect was hurting my lower back.

Mr. Marvelous tilted his head to the side.

"What I mean to say is, we ended the last day with you finding fame after fighting with Dr. Electro and Positron. How was the newfound fame?"

"I see. At that point, my life went from cheap meals and solo nights to fancy restaurants and never worrying about sleeping alone. I got a taste of the celebrity life, and I loved it."

"Were there any new endorsements?"

Mr. Marvelous shook his head. "It was unbelievable. Everyone wanted a piece of me. Toy companies were a big thing. They made several fantastic or should I say—Marvelous action figures."


Mark raised his eyebrows. "He said that?"

Chaz smiled. "Yeah."


"I had a couple of those action figures. I lost two of them. One of them was stolen by a classmate when I was in elementary school." I sucked my teeth.

Mr. Marvelous laughed. "They were popular—at the time. I made a lot of money from the licensing. Then there were the different clothing companies, food products, stores, and restaurants."

"I would like to get back to the action figures."

"Sure."

"I'm guessing you gave permission to use your likeness for the action figures, but what about your rogues gallery? How did that work?"

"The villains didn't have any rights."

"No?"

Mr. Marvelous shook his head. "They forfeited any and all rights once they broke the law," he snarled.


"Well that sucks," Mark said.

"How so?"

"Their identities are being taken and exploited."

"Yeah," Chaz nodded, "but they were lawbreakers. Plus, they were trying to exploit The City and its civilians."

"I guess but...it doesn't seem right." Mark paused. "What if they turned their life around like he said about Dynamo? Should those companies still get to make money off of her image even after she served her debt to society?"

"I don't know. It's not like their action figures are selling anymore."

"Yeah. I'm not saying they should essentially get paid for committing crimes or anything like that, but...there should be some kind of limit to how long a company could do something like that. Imagine if some company could make money of your likeness and story every couple of years."

"Man...I don't know. I don't have the answer for you and I didn't get that deep with Mr. Marvelous. Maybe I should have. I could have gotten his opinion on the matter." Chaz scratched his head. "He probably would have agreed with the toy companies but who knows."

"But that's in the past," Mr. Marvelous continued. His eyes narrowed. "Which ones did you own?"

"I had a Mr. Marvelous one of course."

He nodded. "Naturally."

"The other two were Killer Gorilla and The Meridian. I really liked The Meridian. I never knew what he could do, so I just made up things. He didn't come with any weapons like my Killer Gorilla. Then that stupid kid stole it when I went to lunch with my Grandfather."

"There's a funny story about The Meridian. He was first seen —"

"How long were you two talking about toys?" Mark asked.

"They're action figures," Chaz said. "We were probably talking for another thirty minutes."

With lips tucked, Mark shook his head. "Oh man." He exhaled. "Please skip ahead."

"You sure? He had some really good stories about Killer—"

Mark waved his hands to the question. "No way. I don't want to hear about a super powered hero beating on some gorilla. What happened after that?"

"Ok. I'll skip it, but you are really missing out."

Mr. Marvelous walked over and handed me the album that sat in his chair. "Turn to the first page," he said. There was a picture of Mr. Marvelous at the head of a banquet table. Everyone was facing the camera, so it made it easy for me to get a good look at them, but I didn't know anybody in the picture except for Julie Ambers.

Mark snapped and pointed. "She was in Last Ride of Otter's Ferry; the red head."

"One of the biggest actresses at the time. She was sitting at his side."

"Did you ask about her?" Mark continues, "She had some nice tits. Too bad they never last. That's why you have to catch them young."

"Why do you have to talk that way every time a woman is involved?"

"Is it because I said tits? I'm joking with you. But I do like a nice pair of breast. What's wrong with that?"

Chaz glanced around the restaurant.

"Ok. I'll stop. Did you ask about her?"

"I did but he told me about the others at the table first."

"How many people were at the table?"

"Twenty or so." Chaz silently counted the attendees on his hands. "I think it was around twenty."

"Tell me the biggest names."

"I figured you would say something like that. I'll just give you two; Matthew Torres and Chuck Croger. Both of them were baseball players for the Parkville Wrens."

"I know those two guys." Mark leaned forward. "My father would talk about them all of the time. You know," he said. "Matt and Chuck would get drunk, one or two hours before each game, and still managed to keep it together while playing." Mark stroked his chin as he reminisced. "I remember he told a story about the time he was at a game between the Wrens and the Hounds, and Chuck was throwing up in center field during the second inning; I mean really letting it all out in the middle of the field—and he still managed to catch that fly ball."

Chaz grimaced from the thought. "That's nasty."

"Hey, if you can't handle your drinks, don't go to the bar."

"Yeah." He tucked his lips. "So anyway...at the time of the picture, Mr. Marvelous said he hadn't tasted a single drop of alcohol yet, but those two guys got really hammered by the end of the party. They had everyone at the table in stitches too. He seemed like he really admired them."

"They were the heroes of the sports world; at the time anyway. I'll tell you some stories I heard about them one day."

"Sounds good to me, just leave out the puking," Chaz said. "After I finish this interview, I'm going to need a break from telling stories. You can take over after that." He leaned back in the seat. "So, yeah. After he told me about all of the people at the table, I asked him about the scarlet beauty."


"Is that Julie Ambers?" I pointed at her in the picture.

He walked closer and peered over the book. "Oh yes, that's Ms. Ambers," Mr. Marvelous agreed." She was a talented actress and very beautiful."

He smelled like water and salt. "How did you meet Julie Ambers?"

"I was invited to a party." He cleared his throat. "That kind of thing started to happen quite frequently."

"That's right. You became really popular around this point." I tried to ease the next question with extreme care. Sometimes people don't like to talk about past relationships or certain people. "The way you two are sitting—was this a one-time thing, or did you two become a couple?"

"Hmm." His throat rumbled like a double bass. He then stood up straight. "Let's not do that story yet. That would be jumping too far ahead." He moved to the door as if he knew someone was coming.

"Throughout the day Mr. Marvelous had moved at a normal speed, but for that one moment I got to see him in action. In a flash, he moved from the windows to the door of his apartment. It had to have been at least fifty feet." Chaz rocked his head, squinted his eyes. "I couldn't really see him move that fast, but I did feel the outcome. A second later, the wind from his movement ruffled the papers and my shirt. He was unbelievably fast."

Mark raised a single eyebrow, picking at the crumbs on the wrapper.

The door opened and in walked a young woman. Her heels clacked against the floor with every step. I turned my head so I could see her, but the pillar blocked most of my view. They greeted each other with a smile and a kiss on the cheek. Then, she walked across to his bedroom, picking up a bag from the table along the way. She was dressed in this French maid costume. She forcefully pulled open the metal framed sliding doors with a moan. I know it wasn't supposed to be sexual, but all my ears could hear was the sounds of pleasure.

I cleared my throat. "Who's that?" I asked.

"That's my neighbor," Mr. Marvelous said with a smirk. "She comes around and helps... from time to time." He walked over and leaned against the pillar.

"Oh."

"I could put in a good word for you. She's good at household duties." His eyes narrowed. "I use her services all of the time."

"No. I can't."

He smiled. "Well, if you ever change your mind, let me know. And don't worry, I can keep a secret."

I took one more look at her. She kneeled down on the rug to plug in the vacuum cleaner. The act exposed her panties. As soon as I saw them I turned away.


"You're telling me you didn't look," Mark said.

Chaz wiped his mouth.

"Really?" Mark waited but Chaz stayed tight-lipped. "I hate you." He threw a couple of balled up napkins at Chaz. "As soon as the story starts to get good."

"Alright," he said, pushing the napkins to the side. "She was wearing a pair of black sheer panties." Chaz fell in a trance as he recalled the sight. His mouth drifted open.

"How did it look?"

Mark's question snapped him back to reality, but it only lasted for a moment. "Amazing," Chaz said. He looked out of the window. "Her legs were long and lean—but strong, like a tennis player." He nodded as he reminisced. "She had on these heels." Chaz used his thumb and middle finger to demonstrate the length. "They were six inch high platform heels. And not the clunky, gothic kind either. They had a shine to them like—like um... Do you remember Mary Jane shoes? What are they made of?"

"Patent leather?"

"Yeah." Chaz nodded. "They shined like patent leather and had a tiny red bow on the back of each. I think her toes were out too."

"Did she have on tights or anything?" Mark took a nibble from the rest of his muffin.

"Nope. There was nothing but smooth brown skin. The outfit was a two piece too, so I could see her lower back. She had some kind of tattoo, but most of it was covered by her top."

"Oh man...It must have been good the way you're talking. What happened next?" Mark rubbed his hands together with a devious grin.


Mr. Marvelous walked back over to his chair and said, "Ask me another question before your nose starts bleeding."


"Before your nose starts bleeding?"

"Oh, um—It's a Japanese thing," Chaz said.

"I know that. But why would he say something like that?"

Chaz thought for a moment. "You know—that didn't come to mind when he said it. I did look back into the bedroom though. She was cleaning the bed, lining up the sheets, and stacking the pillows. As I watched her, my imagination—kicked into full gear. There was something about her." His brow furrowed. "I've never had the best imagination when it came to stuff like that. But for some reason, with her, on that day, I could see myself having my way with her. We were doing everything." His eyes grew distant. "All the things I would normally do with Tracy and everything I've been afraid to ask for; she was letting me do it all. And she loved it as much as I did."

"You undercover perv."

"I'm telling you what you want to hear."

"Right. I just want to hear you admit it." Mark scratched the back of his head. "Since you brought it up...What kind of things are you scared to ask Tracy to do?"

Chaz tucked his lips.

"Don't be like that. We were just starting to make a break through."

Chaz let out an exhale and looked around the deli.

"Come on...Don't shut down now."

"Ok, but I'm not telling you everything." He looked around a little bit more to make sure no one was eavesdropping, then leaned over the table. "I've always like the idea of role-playing."

"Role-playing?"

"Yeah. Like playing doctor and patient or—"

"French maid," Mark said as he grinned.

"See...This is why I don't say anything."

"Awww. Are you embarrassed?" he mocked. "You're whispering like you're in to being dominated. I mean...," he grinned again, "it's nothing wrong with that either."

Chaz nodded to himself. "I just don't think she would be interested in dressing up and acting out a scenario with me, let alone wear some kind of lingerie. I think she has a great body, but she never wants to show it off. She might be too self-conscious about her—"

"Uh-huh. I just looking for an overview." He readjusted in the booth. "Let's get back to the story."


She was still cleaning his room, and I was still fantasizing about her body.

"I'm sure she is better than anything you could dream up." Mr. Marvelous' voice crashed into my daydream, ending it abruptly.

"I wasn't..."

"I'm sure you weren't." Mr. Marvelous eyes narrowed.

"Bye." Her voice came from behind me. I looked back into the bedroom. Her image slowly faded like a mirage in the desert. My daydream was ending, but I didn't want it to stop. I turned to get one last glance of her before she had left out of the door for good. "Bye, bye Chaz," she said before closing the door. That's when I noticed. The whole time she was there, I was either seeing the back of her, or her face was covered with her hair.

"It was Jessica," Chaz exclaimed. Mark's smile disappeared and his face became stone. "When I saw her face—I couldn't believe it. She looked amazing the other day but—in that French maid outfit..." Chaz didn't notice the change in his attitude, he just kept talking. "I had some questions about her, but I never got the chance to ask."

"You two know each other?" Mr. Marvelous asked.

"Sort of. We—"

"I get it. Some of the ladies who frequent here are usually very popular." He winked. "Where was I?" He paused for a second. "Women." He grinned. "Right after the women, came the partying, and the drinking."

"Were you doing anything besides drinking? People have said that you were blowing through lots of money and that—"

"Your wife will be calling soon. We will end it here for today."

"I haven't been here for—" Then, all of a sudden, I heard Tracy's voice creeping into the room.

"How much time do you have left?" Her voice growled from behind. I knew she wasn't there, but when I heard her voice, I still turned to look for her. Next thing I remember is being back in the hallway, facing away from the door, with my cell phone still in hand.

"Something's wrong," I said out loud.

"There were these three teenagers—just standing there, together, by the stairs. They were staring at me while they conversed. Just staring...I could only hear whispers flying back and forth between them, but I could tell they were talking about me. I wasn't upset by that. People like to run their mouth, but you can't let that bother you. You know?" He looked at Mark for a brief second before he continued. "I did feel uncomfortable though. There was this weird vibe in the hallway. Something was wrong or off, but as hard as I tried to figure it out, the harder it was for me to concentrate." One moment, Chaz's face was as puzzled as a fresh Rubix Cube, the next, as calm as a sleeping baby. He continued the story.

"You aren't going to answer me now?" She questioned.

"Huh?"

"You haven't been listening to me?"

"Uh..."

"How far are you? I am not trying to stay up another hour. I have to go to work in the morning. Are you trying to get me fired?"

"I'm sorry. I got this weird feeling."

"Enough of the apologies," she said. "When are you going to be here?"

"I am on my way right now. The taxi just pulled up."

# CHAPTER SIX

## Humble pie

Chaz made it home as fast as he could. "My house is right here on the right. You can let me out behind that blue van."

The driver had been too focused on following the car's GPS to listen to any of Chaz's directions. He continued to drive until the GPS told him to stop, which turned out to be two houses down from Chaz's actual residence.

"That will be twenty three dollars even," said the driver, his fingers barely extending through the partition. Chaz didn't have time to get upset. He paid his bill and zipped to his house.

The street was quiet in the cool night. Every surface glistened in the street lights from the drizzle hours prior. He swung open the waist high gate in front of his house, not bothering to close it back up. He would take care of it in the morning. He climbed the stairs while holding onto the railing. It was wet like everything else.

# MAGNANIMOUS ABSOLUTION

Before pulling his keys out of his pocket, he wiped the water onto his pants leg.

Chaz creeped through the front door, placing his set of keys on the console table in a willow basket that housed their mail. The first floor was dark except for the flood lights that filtered through the vinyl blinds in the living room. Its rays barely reached the hallway near the door. His wife, Tracy, sat in a chair facing the door. It was one of the wooden chairs from the dining room set. He could see the marks across the hardwood floor leading to the back of the house. On a normal day, he would have started complaining; "Do you know how much the floor cost? How are we going to get a good price for the house if you keep lowering the value," or something like that.

Slowly, he wiped the soles of his shoes on the door mat. Tracy sat in silence, legs crossed and arms folded. She was already prepared for bed, dressed in the cotton pajamas he bought her for Christmas last year. Since that day, she wore them every night from the middle of fall until the beginning of spring.

Before he could speak, she stood and walked up the stairs to the bedroom, slamming the door behind her. Chaz took off his jacket, hung it on the front door's hooks, and trailed her up to the bedroom. He stopped before trying to enter.

"I'm sorry." He loosened his tie and unbuttoned the top two buttons on his teal cotton shirt, waiting for her to respond. "I didn't realize it was so late," Chaz continued. "I went there right after work. I told you about it the other day." He paused in-between each sentence waiting to hear something back from her. "I thought I told you about it. We were talking, and the time just got away from me."

Chaz twisted the cold metal knob; it was locked. "Talk to me," he pleaded. "Give me a chance to explain myself." He reached out to knock, stopping inches from the door. His head twisted like a dog hearing something queer. "Is she crying," he whispered. He placed his ear to the door; hearing nothing but silence coming from the other side.

Chaz hated to be ignored. To him, being ignored was worse than being slapped in the face, and she knew that. He talked to her about it several times while they were still in college. "We have to talk through our problems," he would say. She would just nod and smile, but it would stay the same. If an argument did happen, she would leave, only to come back when she felt better. When Tracy would finally return, she wouldn't want to rehash the topic. "It's just going to piss me off again. Let's move on." Her parents were her blueprint to handling arguments. They would go through the same process; yelling, separation, reconnection, and then everything was back to normal.

He yanked on the doorknob several times to no avail. "Say something," he commanded. He regretted saying the words the moment they burst from his mouth.

"Goodnight," she said calmly. Her voice barely resonated through the wooden door.

"I'm sorry," he said.

"Goodnight," she repeated.

"I didn't mean to yell at—"

"Good. Night." Her voice echoed through the hallway as if she was standing right beside him.

Chaz sighed; his hands and brow pressed against the door. "Goodnight, and sweet dreams." He turned away defeated, placing his back against the door. He slid down to the carpeted floor where the air was much cooler.

He took off his shoes and tossed them down the hallway. They both bounced before hitting the wall. He resigned himself to stay there until the morning. "I'm not going anywhere until I speak to her," he whispered to himself.

They had a loveseat he could sleep on in the living room, but the last time he slept on it, he woke up with shoulder and back pains. The cushions became more and more malleable over the years from all of the use. Now-a-days, there wasn't enough support to spend much time on the loveseat without something hurting.

Chaz woke up sprawled across the floor; half of his body in the hall and the other half in the bedroom. His throat was like sandpaper. "I need some water," Chaz said with a low, raspy voice. He staggered to his feet, his eyes half open. His hands fumbled at the door frame, clutching at the sides to help him with his ascent. The smell of coffee and bacon permeated the house. As he inhaled the smells of the morning, the aromas gradually revived the rest of his senses, and his grogginess evaporated. He made his way to the kitchen to see if there was anything left for him to munch on.

Tracy stood in front of the slide-in stove, still dressed in her night clothes, making an omelet with strips of sizzling bacon.

"Good morning," Chaz said, testing the waters.

She had never been a morning person, but last night's situation could have made things worse. Her mouth stayed shut. She continued to poke at her meal with the metal spatula. It scraped across the surface of the non-stick pan. The sound made his left eye twitch. Chaz decided to not make things worse by addressing it. "How did you sleep?" He said. "The floor wasn't too bad. I would have been hurting," he said while rubbing his lower back, "if I would have slept on the loveseat. That thing has been falling apart. We should get some new cushions."

Tracy switched the stove off. "I don't know if I did," She said with a sigh. She pushed the omelet off of the pan and onto the empty plate that sat on the island in the middle of the kitchen. "I was up until five in the morning waiting on you—then all you did was snore all night." She looked up at him briefly before sitting down to eat.

Chaz camouflaged his grin by licking his lips. "I'm sorry about that. I tried to sleep sitting up the whole time." He walked into the kitchen towards the stove. The stove was on the opposite side of the island's counter. He grabbed up the pan and spatula and placed them into the double sink that was on the opposite side of the kitchen. He turned on the hot water faucet. "I really thought I told you about the interview last night. I didn't know it was going to take that long."

"And where did you go for this interview?" She asked in between bites.

Steam rose up from the scalding water as it filled the sink, covering the dishes. "I was at Mr. Marvelous' place across town. It was my first time meeting him, so that's why things might have run a bit long."

"Might have?" She paused. "Where were you?" She asked again while chewing on a strip of bacon.

"I just finished telling you. I was with Mr. Marvelous."

She slapped the counter. Greasy prints marked where her hand struck. "Where were you and Mr. Marvelous?"

Chaz frowned after hearing the same question again. "I just told you," he said pausing between each word.

Tracy's teeth clenched. The fork dropped from her hand, clanking against the plate and metal counter top before it crashed down to the floor. "Just say it. You were at the docks." She shifted around on the stool to face him.

Chaz turned off the water before turning around to her. "Yeah, but I was interviewing—"

"You were at the Lofts—and instead of you telling me, I had to find out from Mark." Her head rocked back and forth as she talked. "I shouldn't have to ask around to find out where you are."

"That's what you're upset about? Because I was at the docks?" Chaz leaned back against the sink. His head cocked to one side.

"Why do you keep lying to me, Chaz?"

"What are you talking about? I didn't lie."

"Yes, you did."

"When?"

"You lied by omission. That's even worse."

"How? I forgot." Chaz crossed his arms. The steam from the sink singed the back of his neck.

"You didn't forget. You didn't tell me because you knew how it would sound," she said.

"You always think something is going on."

"I wouldn't have to think that if you would tell me the truth. How am I supposed to trust you?"

"This is exactly it. No matter what I do. What happened was a long time ago, and I didn't even do anything."

"And yet you still feel like you need to lie to me."

"I didn't lie. I thought I told you." His shoulders flinched in pain from the hot steam. He readjusted himself, sliding down the counter away from the sink. "But even if I didn't. Even if—I thought to myself, I'm not going to tell my wife because she isn't going to take it the right way, which I didn't. It doesn't matter because at the end of the day, I'm not your child. I am a grown man. I haven't had a curfew since high school, and I'm not going to revert back to having one now because we're married. If I'm out until three in the morning, then I'm out until three in the morning. I don't have to check in, and I don't have to ask for permission. If you have work in the morning, and you need your nine hours of sleep to be well rested, then go to sleep. Stop trying to blame me for you staying up. If you're going to be mad—be mad when I don't show up, not when I show up later than you think I should."

Her mouth opened from surprise. "Who are you talking to like that? Have you lost your mind?" Tracy exclaimed with a ferocity that Chaz hadn't heard since their first couple of months of dating. She'd always been a passionate woman, and that passion put their relationship on the ropes several times. She would normally try to leave before she got to this point. Last night would have been enough space and time for her to lower some of the tension, but with her lack of sleep and Chaz's habit of always poking the bear, it wasn't able to happen. She launched herself off the stool. It tipped over from the force and crashed on to the glazed ceramic tile.

Chaz nonchalantly sucked his teeth.

She aggressively closed the short distance between them. "Don't try to turn this on me. You're the one in the wrong right now. I wanted to know where you were because I was concerned. I am your wife, and I should be able to know that my husband is still alive and breathing. You could have been dead in a ditch somewhere."

He stood up straight, preparing himself to defend against any impromptu physical attacks. "Accusing me of cheating is not you showing concern for my well-being. I've never cheated on you in the first place. That was all those other guys. Not me," Chaz spewed.

"Those other guys? Really?" Tracy's head recoiled. She shifted her weight. Her shoulder length hair swung in the same direction. "What do you call spending the night over your ex's house?" Her breathing became heavy and turbulent.

Chaz let out a heavy exhale. "We didn't do anything," he said with more restraint, "okay."

"I don't know that."

Chaz's anger flared right back up to the level it was before. "You would know that if you would listen to me instead of your friends."

"You had no business being over your ex's house. Period."

"Where was I supposed to go? You kicked me out of the apartment," he protested.

"You have friends, right?"

Chaz shook his head. "I don't even know why we are going through this again. Nothing happened then, and nothing happened while I was with Mr. Marvelous. Every time I go over there we only talk about his life."

"How many times have you been there?"

"For about a week now."

"A week?" Her hands tightened. "This is what I'm talking about. It takes me a whole week to find out what is going on in my husband's life."

"What are you talking about? You called me the day I went."

"I called you a bunch of times, Chaz." Tracy turned around and picked up the stool, placing it upright on all four legs. "And you finally answered last night—at 4 in the morning while you were at the docks. But, I'm the one that's wrong." She sniffled. "At first—I thought you were busy at work." She wiped at the bottom of both her eyelids. "Some huge project." She sat down on the edge of the stool, her head tilted down. "But you were down at the Lofts," Tracy whimpered, brushing her hair out of her face. She looked back up at him, tears trickled into streams down her cheeks, collecting at her jaw.

Chaz couldn't stand to see her cry. He was angry and wanted to stand his ground, but he didn't think it would go this far. "I'm sorry TC."

He walked over to her with his arms open. She stood up for his embrace. He wrapped his arms around her shoulders, pulling her face first into his chest. With her arms under his, she gripped the back of his shoulders, sobbing. They slowly rocked back and forth, enveloped in each other. They hadn't been this close in months.

"I'm so sorry. I wasn't trying to make you cry." He rested his head on hers. "I felt like I was under attack." Chaz rubbed her back with both hands while still rocking her. "I never want to see you cry—you know that. I swear to you, I thought I told you before I went to meet him the first day."

Tracy pulled him in tighter.

"But you are right. I should've updated you. You're my wife, and you are important. I don't tell you that enough." He brushed through her hair. "Once this is all over, it'll be just me and you. I'm going to take off from work for a couple of weeks, and we are going to go somewhere. How about some place sunny?" He could feel her nodding her head on his chest. Her crying stopped, but her body was still gyrating with each breath. "I have a few more days with Mr. Marvelous, and then we can relax and get back to us."

Immediately, and abruptly, Tracy's breathing went back to normal. She relaxed her grip and stood up straight, taking a step back from him. Her face was as blank as an empty canvas. She stared directly in his eyes.

Chaz smiled. "Are you feeling better?"

She continued to stare at him, tucking her lips.

"What's wrong?"

She finally spoke. "Yeah," she said, wiping her face with her sleeves. "I need to leave."

Chaz leaned his head to the side to see the clock in the hallway. "Oh, that's right. If you hurry, you'll probably make it on time."

She frowned before kissing him on the cheek. "Bye," she said softly.

"Tell me bye after you get dressed. I'll probably be in here by the time you're finished getting ready. I'm still hungry." He patted himself on the stomach.

She walked out of the kitchen and went back upstairs.

An hour went by before she came back down. Chaz sat on the corner of the love seat, facing the stairs, with a cup in his hands.

He watched his wife as she walked down. She took her time as she descended, holding on to the wooden rail. Her skirt restricted her leg movement and the stockings she wore didn't aid her in traction on the beige carpet.

"You look beautiful today," Chaz said.

She raised an eyebrow, stopping in front of their living room. "That thing is raggedy." The loveseat was not only uncomfortable, it didn't match anything in the room. Its blue-grey slip cover was used to hide the ketchup and other stains from two years ago, but now the cover itself is starting to look the same. "Can you throw that seat out? It's long overdue."

"Yeah." He nodded. "Sure."

Tracy slipped into her heels, picked up her thin strapped purse, and put on her dark blue pea coat. Chaz walked into the hallway.

"Bye," he said, opening his arms wide.

She looked at him for a brief second, wrapped a plaid scarf around her neck, and then walked out the door.

# CHAPTER SEVEN

## The Maestro

"Is everything ok?" Mark asked. A fresh cup of water sat in the middle of the table. He had already ordered, but his food hasn't arrived yet.

Chaz sat down and slid into the booth. For once, Mark was at the deli first. "I should be asking you that. You looked really angry last time," Chaz said.

"Yeah, I got over that a couple days ago. Don't worry about me. What's going on with you and Tracy?"

"We just had an argument. That's all."

"She's been asking about you."

"I saw her last night."

"You saw her last night?"

"Yup."

"Look, I really don't want to be in the middle of this. But—"

"You don't need to be. Everything is fine."

"What are you talking about? You two keep putting me in it. It's either you wanting to hanging out, or it's your wife calling me to find out where you are every couple of hours."

Chaz closed his eyes. He took in a deep breath and rubbed his scalp from his forehead to the nape of his neck. He reopened his eyes with a heavy exhale. "Why would you tell her I was at the Lofts?"

"Because she was worried. What was I supposed to do?"

"It would have been better—if you told her you didn't know where I was. How did she get your number anyway?"

Mark shrugged off his question. "How do you think she got my number?"

Chaz's brow furrowed up.

"Calm down, she called my work phone," Mark said. "She said she hadn't seen you for a couple of days."

"How hasn't she seen me? I go home every night."

"Right. You better be going home."

"What is that supposed to mean?"

"People stray. It happens. I get it. I don't think you're that type, but you are giving off some of the signs."

"Really? She's over exaggerating. Like I said, we talked Tuesday. I saw her that morning, and I was home that night."

"Last week?"

"No." Chaz yawned. "Yesterday."

"Today's Tuesday."

"Alright. I meant Monday. I've been working long hours."

"Come on man, she's been calling me for five days now; since Thursday."

"Right." Chaz shook his head.

"Is something going on?" Mark paused. "You can tell me."

"If something is going on, I don't know anything about it. We just finished talking. Everything was fine once she left for work."

"Ok." Mark nodded. "I'm not going to lie for you, so don't even ask."

"I don't need anyone lying for me. Just let me know if she calls you again."

"Sure," Mark said.

"Can we get to the story now?"

"Yeah. Hopefully this time it's good."


"Welcome," Mr. Marvelous said while standing in front of a pair of floor to ceiling folding glass doors that were fully open. He looked out over The City. The balcony had matching patio furniture; green metal with floral patterned cushions. He turned to face me. "Have a seat." Mr. Marvelous gestured to the chair on his left.

I carefully walked over to the chair; making sure not to miss the small step by the door. The side where his study used to be was now walled off. The wall was lined with bookshelves at two different heights. Each shelf on the first floor was covered with different books of different sizes and thickness. It looked like a law office. At the floor level there were four brown boxes stacked on top of one another. The one at the very top was open. From where I was sitting, the box looked empty.

He had more lights in his place now. Lights dangled about six inches from the bottom of the metal library catwalk. The five of them were spread apart at regular intervals. I couldn't see at all what was on the shelves on the second floor, but it was probably more of the same thing. At the end of the catwalk, closest to the door, there was a spiral staircase that attached to it. Nothing that I could tell changed on the bedroom's side.

"Where do you want to start?" Mr. Marvelous asked.

I thought for a moment. At first, I was going to ask about all of the women; I figured that would keep you excited.

"You know me too well." Mark laughed.

Chaz smiled. "But then I thought—what about The Maestro? The first story my father told me about Mr. Marvelous had to do with the devastation from The Maestro."

"That's probably the only story I remember hearing about," Mark said. "Well, that and all of the women."

Chaz tucked his lips and sharply raised his eyebrows. "Right. Why is that always the first thing everyone wants to bring up?" He shook his head. "Mr. Marvelous saved The City several times over, but nobody wants to talk about that. All they ever bring up is the women."

"It's not like it didn't happen." Mark looked at Chaz. "You don't believe them?"

"I'd rather hear it from the horse's mouth."

"Can you tell me about The Maestro?" I asked.

Mr. Marvelous' hand locked around his wrist behind his back. He strolled over and climbed the winding staircase. "Of course." The metal staircase rang with each step. His hand glided along the top of its polished oak railing.

I followed up my question with another. "Why did they call him The Maestro?"

"It had to do with the way 'it' showed up," he said. He stayed close to the railing as he made his way across the catwalk.

"Alright. So when did this take place?"

"Late November. The temperature was starting to drop below 60's during the day." He leaned over the railing on his elbows. His hands dangled loosely, periodically accompanying his speech with swift gestures. "I've always liked the beginning of autumn. The air is more crisp than usual. Do you feel the same?"

"I like the summer. I don't mind the heat."

He pointed at me. "You must've been born in the summer. It gets too humid here. At one point in my career," he said, "I was thinking about relocating to somewhere further north."

"I didn't know you were thinking about moving. What changed your mind?"

"Julie Ambers. I was infatuated by her." His voice softened as he spoke of her. "She was a real beauty, and powerful; not like me of course, but very commanding. I'm far from the only one she ensnared."

"I remember seeing her in that picture you showed me. She invited you to the party."

"She did." He stood up straight. "You have a—good memory," he said while tapping on his temple. "Most people forget things within a couple of days. Is that why you stopped using your Dictaphone?"

I looked down for my Dictaphone on the coffee table. I vaguely remember putting it down, but it wasn't there and neither was the table.

"I hope you aren't forgetting to write all of this down. You don't want to look back at this moment and realize how you wasted your opportunity." He turned and walked away from the railing. "There was this guy I knew that could do the same thing. He would remember everything he heard for a long period of time, but as soon as he wrote it down he would completely forget. If he kept hearing it, he could remember it word for word. So, to make sure he wouldn't forget, he would tell someone else or speak to himself in the mirror." He walked back over the railing with a book in hand. It looked like his photo album. "Have you ever tried that before?" His eyes narrowed.

"What? Telling a friend?" I glanced down at the book case on the first level.

"No." Mr. Marvelous shook his head. "You wouldn't do that." He gave a relaxed smile. "I was talking about repeating it to yourself in front of a mirror."

"No." My heart was pounding in my chest. "I've never tried that before."

"You should try it. It might work for you too."

"I'll—try tonight."

"Do you think he knows?" Mark asked.

"I don't think so. He never mentioned it again, but I couldn't tell."

"Good." He motioned like he was going to toss the album to me. I raised my hands up in preparation. "Catch." He lobbed the book to me. I lifted my head. My eyes tracked the book as it got closer.

"Did you catch the book?"

"Right before it connected with my hands, Mr. Marvelous snatched it out of the air. He caught it with one hand and placed it in my lap. That scared the shit out of me."

"Wait a minute. He made it down to you before the book did?"

"Yeah. Before I could even get out of the seat he was beside me. One hand was on my chest, holding me in the seat, and the other on the book."

He gave a wink and placed the book on my lap. It was the photo album from the other days. "Ironically, it was a day after the peace talks that took place in The City," Mr. Marvelous said.

I leaned back into the chair to give us a little more personal space. I still had some jitters from the adrenaline kick. I cleared my throat. "Peace talks? What peace talks?"

"You were merely a thought in your mother's heart at the time." Mr. Marvelous narrowed his eyes and stared at me. "But—it wasn't publicized." He turned and walked back over to the window. "They wanted me there to help keep the order while the talks were happening."

"Who were the people involved in the talks?"

He placed his hands behind his back, stuck out his chest, and lifted his chin as he surveyed The City. "It wasn't publicized for a reason. And that would take us off topic."

"I'm not asking for specifics." I waited a little bit for his response, but he didn't say anything. So I tried to convince him some more. "Anything you tell me will be 'off the record'."

Mr. Marvelous turned around. He kept his aristocratic posture. "Secrets aren't secrets if you talk about them." His face was stern and stiff. "The people that were involved are none of your concern, and the conclusion of the meeting didn't affect you. So, once again, you don't need to know who was there or what we talked about. Besides," he said, "you already have a great story right now." His face reverted back to something more pleasant.

I was reluctant to continue with the original topic, but I can only push him but so far. "So, he showed up the day after the 'peace talks'," I said with air quotes. I let a bit of sarcasm slip out from anger. I don't think it was missed by Mr. Marvelous.

"Stop saying that. It's not a he, and 'it' didn't show up by itself," Mr. Marvelous snapped. "The Maestro had a small army. Thousands of them cluttered the streets from the bay to The Square right beside Lover's Fountain." He looked around the room as he continued to talk. His eyes seemed distant. "I didn't make it there as soon as they started their attack. News didn't travel as fast back then. I didn't know anything about them until a couple hours in."

He strolled over to the other chair and sat down on the chair's arm, facing me. "To be honest," he rubbed the back of his neck, "I had been partying through the night, and I had no plans of waking up early." He looked up at me. "By the time I got there, the docks were destroyed and some of downtown. After the incident, The City decided it would be easier to demolish most of the buildings and rebuild."

"Oh. I remember my grandparents telling me that the docks used to look completely different," I laughed. "They used to tell me, stay away from the docks because nothing good ever comes from there. I bet they didn't know you lived here."

Mark laughed, gasping for air every couple of bellows. "God. I can't believe you said that."

"Yeah. After I said it, I was thinking the same thing."

"Man, you slipped up. I would've punched you in the mouth." Mark continued to laugh. "You insulted him and his neighborhood in one sentence."

"Yeah. And that's when he flipped me off."

Mark stopped laughing abruptly. "What?"

"He scratched his eyebrow with his middle finger just like this." Chaz mimicked the movement.

"Jesus. You really got under his skin."

I asked, "What did you see when you got there?"

"Destruction." He bounced to his feet, becoming more animated than I've seen him so far. "The clouds covered the sky in a dark gray haze. Once I heard the news, I flew there as fast as I could, high above the clouds to conceal my approach." He mocked his style of flight; arms extended out in front of him, palms down and hands flat. "I could hear screams of terror in the distance as I approached." His hands moved back and forth as he spoke. "I slowly pierced the vale of the clouds, face first, to survey the area. There were thousands of these—critters... crawling around, all over the debris. Cars were flipped; some of them were on fire. There were shards of glass from toppled buildings all over the ground." Mr. Marvelous'sface went pale. He paced back and forth in the middle of the apartment, staring down at the ground. "It was horrific."

"Where were all of the police?"

"Most of them were dead." He stopped in place and pointed at the album. "Turn to the first page."

I opened up the album, and there on the first page was a picture of the Downtown Police Station. It looked like the way it does now, except without the monument. Most of the building was still standing. The buildings around the station on the other hand weren't as lucky. In a semi-circle around the front of the station, there were cement barricades that had sandbags behind them for reinforcement. I continued to flip through the pages. Each picture was taken from a different angle. Most of them were of the Police Station. The other pictures showed all of the devastation that happened in The Square.

"Well, that's what I found out when it was all over," Mr. Marvelous continued. "The police were probably overrun in an instant. There were some barricades made, but it didn't hold any of them back. Those critters climbed right over them.

"Wow. So what happened next?"

"I flew down to help clear out the critters from the inside of the police station. I snuck in through the roof. There was a skylight right above the main hallway. From there, I had access to the rest of the building. I needed to get more information about the situation and the best people to get it from was the authorities. I took my time—searching each floor from top to bottom. I saw the first officer two floors into my search. He was under his desk, laying on the ground, his arms wrapped around his knees. Fear had him frozen in place. I shook him a couple of times and waved my hand in front of his face. All he did was blink."

"Did he survive?"

"I believe so."

"You didn't take him with you?"

"No." Mr. Marvelous shook his head. "I didn't take him with me. I left him right where I found him. He would have caused me more problems than solutions." He looked back at me. "I did make sure there was no danger nearby before moving along." He continued to pace. "So far, I hadn't seen a single one of those critters close up, alive or dead. It looked like there was a firefight, but the outcome of the battle could only be read by the outside of the building.

"What do you mean?"

"There were no bodies, bullet casings, no blood, signs of struggle, or anything," he replied. "I went down two more floors, and I still didn't see anyone else. I started to believe that the officer was the only person left. But when I got down to the first floor, I saw the aftermath of the battle. There was a lot of blood splashed everywhere; over the walls, desks, benches, windows, cubicles. All of it looked like human blood, thick, and dark red, but with a fresh smell." His nose flared as he sniffed around the room. "I could smell something else. I sniffed around as I stepped, creeping between each desk to make as little noise as possible. As I got closer to the basement stairs, the smell grew stronger."

He stopped in place and absentmindedly stroked his nose. It looked like he was trying to remember something. Maybe it was a small detail or perhaps he thought he might have forgot to mention something.

Mr. Marvelous continued, "I remember the weapons locker was in the same direction." He nodded to himself, his brow furrowed. "The room's walls were all thick slabs of concrete. It also had strong bars and metal plates that could help with holding off an attack. I thought that someone might have barricaded themselves in there.

"You would probably go deaf from firing a weapon in there," I remarked.

He nodded. "If anyone was held up in that room, they didn't make it. The back wall behind the metal plates had been destroyed. Those critters would have caught whoever that was in there by surprise and dragged them from their weapons. I made my way down the stairs towards lockup. The basement smelled like rotting fish or sewage. The closer I got to lockup the stronger the smell became. I found three more officers, the captain, and two baby blues huddled in a corner. They managed to lock themselves in one of the cells before getting attacked. In front of the cell was one of those critters laid out on the floor, lifeless, with a claw locked on one of the bars. They were ecstatic to see me," he said. "The two young officers, speaking over each other, told me about the critter and how it tried to break through the bars, bending two of them but not being able to fit through. They had to use all three of their guns to put it down, and they stayed near the corner just in case another one showed up."

"What kind of guns did they have?"

"They had a couple of six-round pea shooters, standard armament at the time. They also said that most of the bullets were bouncing off of its shell."

"Did you get a good look at the critter?"

"I did. I ripped the door off of the cell with one hand. It clattered against the opposite wall. The captain and his two terrified baby blues bounded from the cell. I kneeled down beside the critter." Mr. Marvelous kneeled, reenacting the scene. "The captain was to the left of me." He gestured to his left. "He began to tell me about their situation, what had happened to the precinct, and how this calamity initially occurred to The City. The other two officers, not willing to take a chance with the critter, stood near the opposite wall. I halfway listened as I examined the critter's body." He poked at an invisible body, tilting his head to look at it from different angles. "Its shell, cracked with three holes in what I assumed was its face. Blood oozed out of its fresh wounds onto the concrete. The critter's blood was a blue that I've never seen before in the wild. It looked vibrant and waxy, like a melted crayon."

"Wait a minute. Why does he keep calling them critters?" Mark asked.

"I know. It's not the best name, but I didn't come up with it. I like the term 'brood' more. It doesn't really fit with what they looked like, but 'The Brood' sounds more menacing."

"So, what did they look like?"

"He showed me a picture, but I couldn't keep it or make a copy. But I can still remember how they looked."

"Ok..."

"Try to picture this. What's the most terrifying spider you can think of?"

"I don't know," Mark sighed. He tapped his fingers on the table. "Jumping spiders."

"Nope."

"Tarantulas?"

"Nope," Chaz said with a grin on his face.

"We're playing a game or something?" Mark sneered.

"No, I just thought you would have guessed it."

"What is it?" Mark said sharply.

Chaz leaned in closer over the table. "Daddy Long Legs." He returned back to his position. "Can you imagine a Daddy Long Legs with a body the size of a shopping cart and large crab claws? There were thousands of them crawling around the middle of The City."

Mark raised his eyebrows. "Really? Terrifying?"

"Yup," Chaz said. "War of the Worlds except with huge spiders. They aren't as tall either," he nodded, "but I think you get my point."

"First off, they aren't scary—at all. Second, they aren't even spiders."

"Yes they are."

"No, they're not."

"Yes they are. You can ask anyone here."

Mark surveyed the deli. "Hey." He reached over and tapped a man on the shoulder. The loner was sitting by himself at the counter. "Excuse me. I have a quick question." He spun around on the stool to face them. "Are you scared of Daddy Long Legs?" Mark asked.

He shook his head lightly. "No," the man responded.

"That's only one person," Chaz remarked.

"Alright. Now, are Daddy Long Legs spiders?" Mark asked.

The man combed his fingers through his full auburn beard. "Not that I know of." He waited a moment for a follow up question. When there was none, he turned back around to his meal.

"Cellar Spiders." A woman, three seats down from the man and right next to Frank chimed in. Chaz and Mark turned to see who spoke. The woman looked skinny and short; dressed in a pair of baggy camouflage pants and a large jean jacket with flowers and peace & love patches. She walked over to Chaz and Mark's booth. As she got closer, her height lengthened, now looking taller than both of them in her rugged black platform boots. She stopped at Chaz's side of the table. "What you're probably talking about is a Harvestmen. Most people get them confused," she said while smiling.

"See Chaz. Nobody is scared of Daddy Long Legs except for you and eight-year-old girls."

"Interestingly enough," she said. Chaz and Mark look back at her confused. "Both are called Daddy Long Legs, but they're from two totally different families, Pholcidae and Opiliones," she continued, "There are people who think that they are extremely poisonous." She giggled, "but that's not true either."

"Oh. I didn't know that," Mark said, eyebrows raised. He looked at Chaz for help. Chaz shrugged his shoulders.

"The Harvestman doesn't have venom at all. In fact, their bites can hardly puncture human skin. There by," she pinched the back of Chaz's hand before continuing, "stopping the flow of venom that might have passed through the epidermis."

"Yeah. Thanks for that, um," Mark said to her, his attention still on Chaz.

"Sherry. My name is Sherry." She beamed as she looked back and forth at the both of them.

"Nice to meet you, Sherry," Chaz said politely, "My name is Chaz." They shook hands. The back of her hand was soft and smooth. The inside of her hand was different. It was rough and callused. She smelled like summer.

"Right—thanks a lot, Sherry," Mark interjected, "We appreciate the information." He extended his hand for a shake.

"Oh. You're very welcome," she said while staring into Chaz's eyes. "If you have any more questions, you can let me know." She tucked some of her curls behind her ear. "Any time."

Mark retracted his hand. "Ok, Sherry. We're going to get back to our conversation now. It was really nice to meet you."

"It was really nice to meet you too, Chaz."

Chaz smiled and nodded. She sauntered back to her seat. He watched as her hips swayed with each step.

"What are you doing?" Mark asked.

"Huh?" Chaz's head snapped back around.

"We were just talking about this."

"Talking about what?" Chaz shook his head.

"I'm not going to lie for you, and I'm damn sure not going to sit back and watch you fuck up."

"Sherry?"

"Yeah. Sherry."

"Right. It would be no problem if it was you, though."

"I'm not the one that's married."

"All of a sudden I can't talk to anyone because I am married?" Chaz tapped his hand on his chest.

"I'm not saying anything like that. You—"

Chaz pointed at Mark. "And I'm supposed to take advice from you?"

Mark inhaled deeply before opening his mouth to speak. A waitress walked up to the table interrupting Mark right before his rebuttal. "Excuse me. Can you please keep it down? You two are disturbing the other customers. If you can't, we will have to ask you two to leave." Mark stayed tight lipped. His eyes were burning a hole through Chaz.

Chaz, unfazed by Mark's scowl, responded to the young lady. "I'm sorry. We were having a small argument. We will keep the noise down." He winked at her.

"Thank you," she said cheerfully and then walked away from the table.

Mark's face didn't change in the slightest through Chaz's exchange with the waitress.

"Calm down," Chaz said. "I'm not trying to piss you off, all right." The tension began to fade from Mark's face. "I'm getting tired of accusations like that being thrown around."

"You're right." Mark raked through his hair with both hands. "I just don't want you to mess things up. You have a good thing going." He laughed to himself. "You don't want to turn out like me, with only your work to come home to."

"Come on now. You have more going for you than that."

"Uh-uh." Mark waved both hands back and forth. "You can stop right there. I was trying to lighten the mood to get back to the story. I wasn't fishing for a compliment."

"All right then. I'll get back to the story."


"After I had the conversation with the captain, I had a better picture of what was going on and what happened to the rest of the force. The critters came from Rocky Beach two hours before I showed up. The others erupted from the subway tunnels."

"Others?"

He held up his last three fingers. "There were three different types that were causing chaos in The City; those critters, The Maestro, and the humanoids. The humanoids had claws like giant mole men that could tear through the concrete and asphalt. It wasn't as many of them compared to the critters, but they did all of the heavy lifting. The captain said they were the ones that ambushed them and they're also the ones that knocked down the buildings. They would go inside of a building and rip at its support columns. After a couple of minutes, the building would collapse, and then they would move on to the next. Those humanoids took down two blocks worth of buildings in less than an hour."

"Did you see it happen?"

"No. All of it was told to me by the captain. By the time I got there, they had all stopped in The Square around Lover's Fountain."

"Like they were waiting for something...," Mark said, eyes squinted.

"Yeah. He said it only took them forty minutes to get to The Square."

"So they were standing around there for what, an hour and twenty minutes?"

Chaz nodded. "They were still tearing things up in that general area, but they weren't moving any further into The City."

"You only personally saw four police officers, where were the rest?"

"He said a few had been killed in the initial push from Rocky Beach. Once the critters got to The Square, They tried to make our stand. Within a couple of minutes, they were over run, and most of them retreated further into The City."

"Did he tell you anything else?"

"No. That was all of the information that he had. They got locked in the cell during the retreat process. After we finished talking," Mr. Marvelous said, "I flew all of them uptown, to safety. I felt confident with all of the information the captain gave me. I was now ready to attack. I flew back to The Square as fast as I could. I landed with a thunderclap in the middle of a couple dozen of those critters. Their body parts exploded from the impact. Pieces of shells, chunks of meat, and blood scattered from my impact." Mr. Marvelous' eyebrows raised. "I created a crater in the ground too." He paused for a moment, then shrugged. "The area was already in shambles, I don't think anyone would've noticed."

He turned around and looked at me. It felt like he was waiting for me to agree but I didn't know what to say. I gave a coy smile.

Mr. Marvelous' eyes narrowed. "Where was I?" He turned back towards the windows. "The landing...the shock of the impact, and the slaughter of their comrades must have terrified them. They all froze in place—as still as a statue, not moving a single inch. All of them, except for The Maestro. He turned to look at me as I stood up. Pieces of their shells stuck to my outfit. Their blue blood dripped down my legs and boots. The smell of sewage came back, filling up my senses with a tremendous stench. It must have been the blood," he suggested. "I wiped some of the blood off of my face with both hands." He stood, with his legs shoulder length apart, and his arms to his side. "We had ourselves an old fashion showdown, standing there in the breeze, the sun creeping to its apex. The Maestro, fifteen to twenty yards away, stood silent on top of the fountain where the statue used to be."

"What did The Maestro look like?"

"The Maestro looked nothing like those critters or the humanoids. Every one of 'its' body parts were in normal human proportion except for 'its' face. 'Its' eyes were like a house cat's; they dominated 'its' face, black as pitch with yellow on the very edges. The Maestro had no hair; 'its' head was as smooth as a concrete ball. 'Its' mouth was like a slit in 'its' face, wrapping all the way back to where an ear would be." Mr. Marvelous marked the area on his own face with his finger. It was wide like a hand puppet. "No lips, ears, nose, or anything of the sort that would otherwise protrude from that area. 'Its' skin was a reddish-brown color, all over. 'Its' hard surface shined like a glossy ceramic."

"I've always thought The Maestro had antennas. I remember somebody telling me that," Mark said.

"Yeah. I feel like I heard the same thing. Tall, thin as a rake..."

Mark joined in with Chaz's description. "...big eyes, long antennas, scaly skin, large hands, and giant fangs."

Both nodded at each other. "So, they were wrong?"

"I guess so," Chaz said. "Both descriptions are close to each other though. Their imaginations must have gotten the best of them on certain details."

"Did you tell him?"

"No. I just let him keep talking about The Maestro."

"'Its' posture looked confident and proud. Then, The Maestro outstretched its arms in a smooth and lofty manner. I watched The Maestro's movements as close as possible," Mr. Marvelous said.

He then showed me what he meant. He first stood there stiff, chest up, back straight, arms locked to his sides. His legs were the same with one heel pressed into the arc of the other foot, forming a 'T'. Then, he gently raised his arms, wrist first, up to his shoulders. The movement was fluid like a ballerina. The rest of his body relaxed with the motion.

"At the same time, the critters all turn to face The Maestro. At that very moment, I knew 'it' was controlling them, but I didn't know what I should do. So I started walking towards The Maestro. I acted as a negotiator for a little. I tried to reason with 'it', calm it down."

"What did you say?"

"I said things like...What do you want? Where did you come from? You don't have to do this. We can work this out. But, The Maestro didn't respond at all or even move. 'It' stood still, in the same posture like a statue until I got more than halfway to it. That's when..."

Mr. Marvelous closed his eyes. His right arm started moving, light and soft motions, like an orchestra conductor. His left arm soon followed with the same lofty motions.

"The humanoids came," Mr. Marvelous continued. "They crept up from behind me while all of my attention was on The Maestro. I didn't hear them at all."

"Wow. This is getting exciting," Mark said. "I feel like I should have a snack to eat right now."

Chaz chuckled. "Imagine how I felt while he was telling me and moving around the room. It was spellbinding."

"What did they do?" I asked.

"Four of them rammed into me and latched onto each of my limbs. It felt like I got hit by a bus. They took me down to the ground. My face sandwiched between the body of one of those humanoids and the cobblestone in the Square." Mr. Marvelous laid down on the ground, his legs stretched to the side, his arms crossed behind his back. "Then they started to pile on me like a Football match. It felt like twenty or thirty of them biting and clawing at my body."

I leaned forward in the chair. "Where was The Maestro?"

"I couldn't tell. There were too many of those critters; they blocked my view. My head was too low to the ground to see past them. But I did have an eerie feeling. I could feel The Maestro getting closer. My plan was to lay there and act like I was stuck, then catch The Maestro by surprise. So, I pretended to be struggling." He shook and wiggled on the ground. "Then, once I thought he was close enough, I erupted from under the pile of his underlings."

He launched himself off of the floor and into the air. He hovered several feet above the ground. I popped up from my seat about the same time. "Their bodies were ejected off of me," Mr. Marvelous said. "But..." He lowered himself back to the ground, touching down lightly. "The Maestro," he continued, "was still at the fountain, standing in the same position, still as an iron flag."

"Did they attack you again?"

Mr. Marvelous nodded his head. "Oh yes. They jumped up after me. Leaping off the back of other critters, they grabbed my ankles and made a living chain. That is also when The Maestro started to move more."


"Here we go," Mark said with a smile. His right leg bounced with excitement.


"The Maestro's hands bounced and waved around." Mr. Marvelous started waving his hands around like a conductor. "The more The Maestro's hands became erratic, the more the critters and humanoids did." He paused for a moment and then looked at me. "The living chain that they created, they began to pull me back down to the ground. The smaller ones climbed up, biting at my neck and head. With all of the extra weight and pulling, they succeed at bring me back down to Earth." Mr. Marvelous shrugged his shoulders. "I'm stronger on the ground than in the air; leverage and all of that. But—that's when the real brawling began. All of the ones that were close enough to me joined in and piled on." He bobbed and weaved through the apartment, punching at the air. His steps were light and precise, liked a young gifted boxer. The air popped with each explosive swing. "I was doing my best to dodge claws and hands that swung for my face and body. Attack and defend." He swung a couple more times. The wind from his punches circulated through the apartment, ruffling my clothes. "Attack and defend."

He continued to prance around the room, moving slow enough for me to follow his movements but fast enough so I could tell, without a shred of doubt, there was no man that could compete with his level of skills and gifts.

"None of them could survive a single strike from me. Each blow ruptured their shells and sent their carcasses flying. I kept swinging and kicking, and they kept coming in droves. I threw a couple of them to create some space, but that didn't work either. Their numbers seemed so endless. I knocked away two or three and ten more would come scuttling in sideways. And while I was dealing with them, I would catch a glimpse of The Maestro, still standing there, waving his hands back and forth; controlling the show from his balcony seat."

"Why didn't he just attack The Maestro?" Mark asked while scratching the top of his head. "I mean, if that's the one running the show—"

Chaz yawned and covered up his mouth. "I'm getting to it," Chaz said with watery eyes. "You going to let me?"

"Yeah... go ahead."

"I needed to stop him," Mr. Marvelous said. "So I cleared a path. I pulled the nearest light pole out of the ground." He wrapped his arms around one of the pillars in his place and did a quick jerk. "I swung the pole like Matthew Torres, aiming for the stands." He mimed holding the pole and swinging it. It was a magnificent. "I knocked tens of them out of the way. I then launched the pole at The Maestro like a javelin, using almost all of my might. It whistled as it sped through the air. My aim was true, and it flew directly at The Maestro's chest. Right before it reached its target, a dozen or more of those critters bunched up in front of The Maestro. The pole stopped after penetrating several of the critter's living shield. They were able to protect The Maestro from my makeshift missile."

"Wow, it didn't work? Did you try again?" I could feel sweat dripping down my back.

"Yes. I tried with another pole and a car. Each time The Maestro would raise ITs right hand and either the critters or the humanoids would take the impact instead. It was frustrating, but it did help me thin the herd."

I tried to ask a question, but I yawned through it. Mr. Marvelous turned around and stared at me. I was a little embarrassed. I don't think yawning through an interview is very professional.

"What did I do next?" Mr. Marvelous asked as if he was trying to interpret my distorted words. "I did the only thing I could think of at the time. If I couldn't get to The Maestro because of his— underlings, I was going to wipe all of them out first."

Mr. Marvelous began to zip around to room. He zig-zagged as he threw a couple of punches and kicks. I had a hard time keeping up with his movements that time around.

"I was exhausted by the time I finished. My breathing was labored, and I could barely keep my eyes open. But I had one more to go before I could stop. I staggered towards The Maestro. My feet grazed the ground with each step." Mr. Marvelous lumbered across the room towards the door. His whole body rocked with each step. "I was like the walking dead."

I slid to the front of my seat. "What was The Maestro doing?"

"The Maestro stood in the same place, on top of the fountain, not moving or talking. I kept moving towards The Maestro, wiping blood from my face and around my eyes. My suit was soaked with their blood." Mr. Marvelous stopped several feet from the door. "I stopped, took in a deep breath, and said, 'It's over. Give up.' All of 'its' fallen comrades didn't seem to effect The Maestro at all. So, I started moving closer. If The Maestro wasn't going to give up, I was going to have to subdue 'it'. Then, The Maestro's hands shot back up—to shoulder level." Mr. Marvelous stood up straight and turned towards me. "I stopped again." He twisted his head from side to side. "I could hear something. The sound was getting louder."

"Oh...Don't tell me," Mark said.

Chaz smiled.

"More of them were coming?" Mark asked.

"Hundreds. They climbed out of the holes that were created by the original humanoids. Some of them were even coming out from the collapsed buildings."


"I was surrounded," Mr. Marvelous shouted. "Their circle of death closed in around me. There was nowhere for me to escape but up, and I was too tired for flight. I had to finish what I started. I put my last bit of energy in to knocking The Maestro out. I made two quick steps and—"


"Hey guys," the server said.

Chaz and Mark turned.

"Sorry to interrupt," he said, "we will be closing down the kitchen in ten minutes. Is there anything you wanted to order?"

"No." They both said simultaneously.

"Are you sure, sir? I know you like to get the chicken wings." He pointed at Mark. "We can get them heated up for you. It shouldn't take long at all."

"I'm not hungry."

"How about you, sir?" He turned to Chaz.

"No, thank you," Chaz said.

"How about dessert. We have some lovely—"

"We're fine with our waters," Chaz insisted.

"I just wanted to—"

"Can't you see we're having a conversation?" Chaz said.

"Relax Chaz." Mark turn back to the server. "I'm sorry about that. We won't need anything."

The server nodded and walked off.

"Thank you," Mark said.

"I hate when people interrupt," Chaz said. "That's so rude."

"You need a break or something."

Chaz rubbed his face and head. "I don't think I've been getting enough sleep." He shook his head. "Where was I?"

"Mr. Marvelous was about to attack The Maestro I think."

Chaz nodded. "Right...Right."


"I made two quick steps to close the distance and swung," Mr. Marvelous said. "It connected. I hit The Maestro squarely on the jaw. 'Its' knees buckled before keeling over." He sat down on the floor across from me; his legs out stretched, his arms propping himself up. "If I wasn't so tired, I probably would have knocked The Maestro's head off. But..." he looked up at the ceiling, "...all those critters that surrounded the area, preparing to pounce—they all stopped in place, went limp, and then collapsed."


"Wow," Mark said.

"I sat down exactly like this. After a couple more minutes, I was lying down." Mr. Marvelous chuckled.

I laughed too. I felt as relieved as he probably did that day.

"Once I opened my eyes again, they were gone and the military was there; helicopters, trucks, and personnel. Now—I'm not talking about their bodies being gone; they were all piled up like hills of death. But the ones that showed up at the end, they were nowhere to be found." Mr. Marvelous climbed up to his feet. "Either the military was lying to me or those critters scattered before they ever showed up." He walked back over to the windows. Storm clouds began to form over the horizon, and the baby blue sky shifted to gray.

"That—that was an amazing story. You had my palms sweating." I laughed, rubbing my hands on my pants. "So, military showed up. Am I correct in assuming that they woke you up?"

He gave a slow nod.

"Ok. So you wake up, meet some of the military, and they're there piling up carcasses. What did they do with The Maestro?"

"He was shipped off with the bodies. They brought a fleet of dump trucks for the bodies. They started with the mostly intact bodies and worked their way all the way down to small pieces of the shells. The Maestro got ITs own truck. It looked like a regular 18 wheeler, but the inside had several different kinds of metal restraints hanging from the walls and a clear plastic box with circular holes at the top for The Maestro to be housed in. After they finished the cleanup, they took The Maestro away. 'It' couldn't be held in a regular prison and at the time; no one fully knew how 'it' was controlling those other creatures. The military decided, with my input of course, to hold The Maestro underground in a secret facility. They placed The Maestro in a sensory deprivation tank and kept 'it' constantly sedated."

"That was a good story; really good actually. You need to bring more of that," Mark said.

"I think they're good all of the time. It might be the way I'm telling the stories." He laughed to himself. "That's why I'm not on TV."

"Here's to hoping your writing is better." They toasted their cups together. Chaz guzzled down the water in a couple of gulps. Mark took a couple of sips and placed it back down on the table. "Did you ask him where the facility was?"

Chaz smiled. "Nope. He didn't want me to ask about that. We ended it there. I told him bye and let myself out."

"I doubt he would have told you but you should have asked. What happened to being a reporter?"

"I know, but he was already complaining when I asked about the meeting."

"But that is a part of your job. Doctors don't pass up on saving a life, and reporters don't pass on asking the hard questions."

Chaz laughed. "Where did you hear that from?"

"I don't know." Mark grinned. "Probably some cop show. It makes sense though."

They laughed together and then became quiet. Chaz looked around the place. It was mostly empty except for a couple of customers at the counter and the employees. The busboy and two of the waiting staff were wiping down the unoccupied tables and seats. The young man he yelled at earlier flipped the open sign on the door to closed.

"Let's get out of here before they lock us in," Chaz said.

"Yep."

They both slid out of the booth, grabbed up their belongings and walked to the front door. The waiter was standing by the door, letting out some of the straggling customers, and locking it behind them. Mark nudged Chaz on his shoulder as they approached.

"Hey man," Chaz said while walking up to the young man. "I'm sorry about that earlier." Chaz slipped him a twenty concealed in a handshake. "I've got a lot of stress going on from work and at home." The waiter hesitated to look at the foreign object in his hand. Chaz placed his hand on the waiter's shoulder. "Please, except my apology."

"Yes, sir."

Chaz smiled, nodded, and followed Mark out the door.

"Whelp," Mark said.

"Thank you, sir," the waiter yelled holding up the folded bill.

Chaz gave him a friendly wave as he continued across the street.

"You paid the kid?" Mark asked. Chaz kept walking. Mark followed one step behind. "Really?"

"I was giving him a tip. He could have made that if we would have ordered something."

"Ass," Mark said.

# CHAPTER EIGHT

## New Blood

Chaz collapsed in the booth with Mark. Not a word spoken between the two of them for over five minutes. Mark stared out the deli's window at the cars passing by. The sun was beginning to set on The City. The sky shimmered with its golden rays.

"It looks beautiful outside," Mark said while nodding. "How are you holding up?" He turned to look at Chaz. Chaz's eyes were halfway open as he stared off into the distance. "Chaz."

"Yeah," he said blinking several times. "I'm sorry. I'm so tired."

"You haven't been sleeping good?"

"No." He rested his head in his hands. "I keep waking up every other hour. I stay awake for a half-hour or so, and then it happens again. Normally I sleep like a rock."

"Have you been having strange dreams? Sometimes I can't sleep because of that."

"I don't remember my dreams. I don't think I've been asleep long enough to have any."

"Hello gentlemen," said the young waitress. "Can I get you something to eat or drink?"

"Hi," Mark said. "Can I have an order of wings?"

"Sure thing. What about you, sir?" She pulled a small note pad and pencil out of her waist apron, prepared to write down his order.

"No food for me. Thanks," Chaz said.

She tucked the stationery back into her apron. "I can get you some coffee or tea."

"He doesn't like caffeine," Mark said.

"I'll drink it today," Chaz chimed in. "Can you bring me some coffee?"

"I'll bring that right out to you and place your order of wings."

"Thanks." Mark stroked his neck. "Maybe you should take something. Have you ever tried melatonin? It could help."

Chaz took in a deep breath, letting it out as slowly as it came in. "No," he said, at the same pace off his exhale. His voice was a raspy low tone. "I'm so tired. The last time I was this tired, it was from being in the hospital all night watching over Tracy, and then going straight to class afterwards. I didn't get to sleep in until she was discharged a week later. I didn't think this was going to happen again until we had children."

"It's probably work."

Chaz looked up, a little more lively than before. "With Mr. Mar—"

"Here's your coffee. Sugar and cream are on the table."

"Thank you," Chaz said with a nod. He pulled the hot cup of joe right under his nose. He sniffed it several times. "With the interview?" He whispered as she walked away.

"Just work. Sometimes I catch up on emails in bed, you know. They say that isn't good for you. The light—I think it confuses your brain on what time it is. So when your body thinks it's time for sleep, the light gives your brain a signal like it's still day time—or something like that."

"That could be it." Chaz sat up straight and poured some sugar into the cup. "I've been doing some research later than usual."

"I've been doing some research too."

Chaz looked up from his coffee. "Don't tell me you've been looking for Dynamo."

"I mean—I wasn't looking for her secret identity."

Chaz tightened his lips and exhaled. He balled up his fists and tapped them on his temples. "What are you doing?"

"I didn't only look for her," Mark replied. "She was the first name, but I looked for his other villains too. I wanted a visual of who he was fighting with. What's wrong with that?"

His hands loosened. "I guess that makes sense." He cooled the coffee with a couple of blows before taking a quick sip. "Who did you find?"

"I couldn't find any photos of Dynamo or The Maestro, but—"

"I told you."

"But," Mark repeated, "I did find some articles on the incidents. One of them talked about how Dynamo destroyed the fountain by throwing a car at Mr. Marvelous."

"A whole car?"

"Yeah, and you know they were heavier back then. Another one said something about—"

"Here's your wings. I put some dipping sauces on the side," the waitress interjected. The aroma of the chicken permeated through the air.

"Oh. Thank you sweetie." Mark waited until the waitress walked away. "She's trying to get a tip."

They both laughed.

"But um...You didn't know about the car thing?"

"Nope." Chaz shook his head as he spoke. "I looked over my collection two days ago. It had nothing but his earlier days fighting low-level crime. Some of them were basic overviews of his life with no real details. It seemed like I had so much more when I was younger."

"Everything seems bigger when you're younger."

Both men quietly smiled and nodded.

"Anyway," Mark said, "the other papers talked about the day The Maestro showed up. There was going to be a parade and a concert in the square that day."

"Really?"

Mark smiled. "You have me looking like the expert over here."

"You missed your calling—snooping on people."

"Researching." Mark dipped the crispy wing before taking a bite. "Damn, this is good."

"You eat the same thing every time you come here."

"Why change something that's this good?"

"You should get some greens every once in a while. You're probably backed up."

Mark laughed. "That's what prune juice is for."

"That's nasty," Chaz said while yawning.

"What did you two talk about this time?"

"Welcome," Mr. Marvelous said, waving me over. This time he was sitting in a chair across from my usual position. It was pouring outside. The curtains were barely cracked, but I could hear the rain beating against the glass as the wind howled. "Have a seat."

I walked over and sat down. The stack of books and papers were back with the photo album sitting on top of the pile. "Been doing some reading?"

"You could say that." He smiled. "I was thinking. I been doing most of the speaking. Maybe it's time I start letting you ask more questions—being as though you're the reporter. So, where do you want to start?"

"I told you," Mark said.

"Yeah." Chaz shrugged. "Both of you were on the same page."

I wasn't prepared for that. I had my opening question but no follow ups. "Tell me about your rival."

"My rival?" He laughed. "We were never rivals." Mr. Marvelous stopped and looked at the floor before commenting again. "Maybe from the view point of the society."

"Well, that is his statue out there, towering in The Square, not yours." He looked at me sharply. I must have been getting ahead of myself.

"It is," he replied.

I pushed forward with my questioning. "Are you saying that you wouldn't want to have a monument of yourself there instead of him?"

"How about we—" he cleared his throat, "take a step back first. Let's talk about how that whole situation started."

"Sure." He gestured to me. I repositioned myself in the chair before I spoke. "When did Solar make his first appearance?"

"He showed up a short while after The Maestro."

"How long is a while?"

"About seven months after I received the key to The City and another parade, this time for saving the downtown area." He pointed at a wall behind me.

The large decorative key hung from the wall in a golden trimmed case. It had a plate at the bottom of it with some writing, but the letters were too small.

"Mayor Malone himself placed that key around my neck. I wore it like a medallion around my neck, everywhere I went, for weeks. Could you believe I actually thought that I could open up something with that key?" He gave a grin. "It was a beautiful day. Thousands of people showed up, and I'm not only talking about people from The City. There were people from all over the country that came for the festivities. As far as your eyes could see, people were cheering and dancing in the streets. There were floats, enormous balloons, acrobats, different kinds of cuisines, fireworks that lit up the sky at night, and even a military air show. The whole weekend was filled up with celebrations."

"My parents told me about it. They called it The Celebration of the Century. They actually met there."

"Oh really?"

"Yeah. They were really young at the time, but both of them have the same picture from the event. My mother came here with her parents and siblings. My father came with his Boy Scout troop. They both took part in the sack race and the three-legged race, boys versus girls; that sort of thing. They got their picture taken together with the rest of the group. What are the odds?"

"Some call that fate."

We both smiled, our minds collectively reflecting back on the past and how things come together.

"What am I doing? I'm sorry. I'm over here telling you about myself again. I should be asking you questions." I cleared my throat. "What happened after the weekend?"

"Everyone went back to their normal lives, but me. I was still riding high. The world was mine; I didn't fully realize it at that moment. Ms. Ambers and I had been going steady for about a year by that point. We had already moved in together."

"Two young love birds, both of you on the top of the world; things must have been great."

"Not quite. While things were good, I was the only hero people cared about, but that novelty started to fade. The Maestro was the biggest villain to sweep through The City in a long time and slowly The City's nature reverted back to what it once was. Small crimes were happening sporadically all over The City. That's when the new guy showed up," He said with a quick grimace. "He started with the low level crimes. They were the types of crimes I would leave for the cops by that time in my career. Most criminals feared me, so it was less likely for anyone to break the law out in the open, and the ones that weren't scared were usually not the most intelligent." He flashed a half smile. "I focused on the bigger threats and disasters."

"Were there any big disasters or threats looming around that time?"

"I wouldn't say so. There was Killer Gorilla and Scorch, but mainly my head was in the clouds. I didn't notice him picking up my scraps while I was away from the table. As he got better at the job, I was getting less invites and phone calls. At the time, I didn't know what was going on, and initially I didn't care. Most of the places they weren't getting in contact with me anymore were becoming less trendy anyway," Mr. Marvelous said. "Some of the individuals, on the other hand, were more important. I spoke to several of them, but they never had any real answers for me, nothing but excuses. Maybe I should have had some idea. The citizens were talking about him, but I wasn't listening," he said. "After I found out, I tried to stay nonchalant. I was still the alpha male of The City. There was no need to waste my time thinking about his movements." He tucked his lips. "I was wrong, obviously. Turns out that he was building a movement that would be the foundation for his rise to fame."

"How long did that go on?"

Mr. Marvelous' eyebrows bunched up. "Him building or me being nonchalant?"

"Solar—building his movement."

"It lasted for eight months. Throughout that time, I guess he worked up his confidence to battle against stronger foes. In no time. He was battling his own crop of villains. Nothing up to my level, but each one would test his limits."

"Can you name some of them?"

"Yes, of course. Let's see..." Mr. Marvelous pondered for a moment. "There was a set of twins that robbed convenient stores throughout The City; The Mosh Twins. Harold 'Truck' Peters was a big fella. That guy ran an extortion and coercion crew; they stayed on the outside edges of The City; and then there was the Pelican."

"The Pelican?" Mark said.

Chaz smiled. "He looked like a Pelican. He dressed up in a mostly white suit with a black cape, and yellow boots. He also had a large pouch around his stomach to hold things he stole."

"That's supposed to mimic the thing on the bird's neck?"

"I don't think he planned that out. People started calling him that because of how he looked while he was soaring across to different buildings. He was considered just a public nuisance. He stole things, but it was usually items that people didn't really need or wanted in the first place."

"So...why was Solar chasing him down?"

"Probably had something to do with public safety. Sometimes things would fall from his pouch when he flew by. About ten people or so received minor injuries over the year." Chaz said, wobbled his hand. "He was one of the only ones that got a nickname."

"That's nothing to be proud about." Mark laughed.

"He's also the only one never to be caught." Chaz sipped some coffee. "Every time Solar thought he had him cornered, The Pelican would make a daring escape off of a roof top or into the water."

"Why didn't you intervene by that time? You knew what was going on with him right?"

"I did," he said. "My attention was pointed in a different direction. I had my lady, my fame, and all of those parties using up every ounce of my time. Why should I care about some vigilante? Why should the citizens care?" He raised his eyebrows. "That's what I thought."

"You were a vigilante," I said.

"To me, he was a vigilante. I was something different. He was a regular guy putting on a costume and beating on criminals."

"Sounds like the exact same thing to me," Mark said.

"I agree, but Mr. Marvelous had a reason why he thought differently."

"I was completely different," Mr. Marvelous explained, "I was powerful and one of a kind. I had the right to enforce the law," he boasted. "I was above everyone. Who else would you want to maintain the rules of the land? Should man judge man, or should that judgment come down from a higher power?"

"He sounds like he is full of himself."

"Yeah, but that's how most ancient societies did it. The people with power were usually the ones setting the laws and dispensing the punishments."

"We aren't living in ancient times," Mark snapped back.

"Yeah, but that's what they did."

"And the people revolted. Those people with power," Mark said with air quotes, "were overthrown by the citizens."

"That's true too. He said he only felt like that for a little."

"Were you trying to rule?" I asked.

"No."

"But you think you had more of a right to uphold the laws than him?"

"Yes." He paused. "I did. If an ordinary man wants to help keep the crime rate down and protect the citizens of The City, then that man could join the police department. He could uphold the law and get paid for it. I was doing more than that. I handled threats that the police department and the military couldn't."

"He was beloved by everyone since the beginning of his career, but you felt differently about him."

"I did. I was young at the time and immature. He was stepping into my domain, and I didn't like the encroachment."

We both fell silent for a moment. I don't know what he was thinking, but I was trying to figure out my next question. I was debating if I should follow up with another question about him ruling or should I just move back to his conflict with Solar. He continued to talk before I could make a decision.

"I didn't have a serious problem with him at the time. Not at all. I didn't want anyone replacing me, and it felt like that's what he was trying to do."

"But from all accounts, from civilians that lived back then and even from you, he was a benefit for The City. He was picking up the pieces that you left behind as you moved to bigger hazards. If anything, he was helping you."

"It didn't feel that way. I felt threatened. He wasn't someone I could challenge in my normal way. I couldn't beat him up; the citizens would hate me for it. Nothing I could have done would have slowed down his momentum."

"I can understand that. You had a place in The City, and you were the only hero for a time being. You gave your blood and sweat to make it as far as you did. It had to hurt when someone new came along and slowly usurp you."

"That's how I felt—at the time. I've garnered a better perspective during these past decades. I realize that wasn't what was really going on. Like you said earlier, he was really helping me. That's why I don't think of him as a rival. To be a real rival, both sides should be in an active conflict with each other. I was the only one with a problem. I'm sure that worked in his favor."


"You're getting a lot more out of him now. You should have been asking him questions like this since the first day." Mark said.

"I know. I know."

"You're like a real reporter now. They might have to start paying you."

"I was star-struck at the beginning, that's all," Chaz said. "You would've been the same way."

"Maybe."

"Whatever."


"So, I didn't like him," Mr. Marvelous said, "but I couldn't ignore him either. I tried. I had my fame to try and drown him out, but it doesn't help when the upper class is talking about him too. And then Ms. Ambers started."

"Started what? Did she start talking about him?"

"Yes. It was almost every day. She would always talk about his costume, gadgets, and the crimes he stopped. I nodded and smiled at first." His nose flared. "She would go on and on about how his body looked in his skin tight suit. I kept telling her it was armor, but she wouldn't stop." His face flushed with blood, eyes darted back and forth. "I can't do this right now." He turned away from me and took a deep breath. His shoulders slumped with the exhale. "I promise I will talk about her. I just can't talk about both of them at the same time. They both had a huge effect on my fame."

"I didn't mean to upset you," I said. Getting him upset was the last thing I wanted to do.

"I know. You were only doing your job," Mr. Marvelous said before turning back around. There were no traces of tears on his face, but his eyes were watery. He blinked several times to clear them.

"Solar started off tackling low level crimes; carjackings, muggings, and misdemeanor theft. Because of that you didn't hear much about him. As time went on, he began to handle more dangerous criminals like gangsters and loan sharks. Is that around the time you really started to hear about his exploits? Or—was it after he began to have his own archenemies?"

"The latter. But, like I have said before, I was exceedingly famous by then. I'm not trying to be arrogant, but if people were talking to me, it was usually about me. I also wasn't in the circles of the ordinary."

"Yep. That's it right there. That's why people revolt," Mark said. "As soon as the people at the top stopped mingling with the rest of the population, they lose a sense of their plight. All they care about is their good times, their money, and their possessions. Then trouble comes and the rest population cries out for help, but they don't hear them. They don't care because they don't see the peril or the plight. Everything is roses where they are. So after that, the people resort to other means to show their frustrations."

Chaz raised his eyebrows.

"What?"

"I just—wasn't expecting that," Chaz said.

"Come on. You know that type of thing gets to me."

"I do now."

"People started talking?"

"Yes. The talk started off causal. Solar's name would get lightly peppered into mundane conversations. A month or so goes by and the next thing I know, they are talking about him all of the time. People actually started asking me about him: did I know him or if I could get in contact with him? It was a slap in the face." His voiced raised ever so slightly. "I'm the one that saved them from certain death. Solar wasn't there to save the day, I was."

"People like mystery."

"What did he do to earn so much adoration?" Mr. Marvelous didn't pay me any mind. His hands flexed as he continued to talk. "He beat up some purse snatchers or saved a couple of cats from trees. A firefighter and a regular beat cop could have did those things. I've saved The City, the whole city, more than once by that point. I was furious." Mr. Marvelous paced around the room. His head tilted down, he stared at the floor. He looked really irritated. "Well," he stopped in place, "that's how I felt at the time." His mood abruptly lit up. "Do you have any siblings?"

"Siblings? No." I shook my head. "I'm the only child."

"I see. I was an only child too. So, you might not be able to relate. Have you ever heard of the term red-headed stepchild? It's an old term."

"Yes, of course."

"I became that red-headed stepchild."


"More like a black sheep," Mark chimed in.

"You weren't there."

"I wasn't." Mark shrugged. "You weren't either."

"So what?"

"I'm not coming up with this on my own."

"Believe half of what you see and none of what you hear," Chaz said somewhat to himself.

"What?" Mark leaned in.

"Eyewitness testimony can get corrupted by personal bias. Plus, people like to slander and gossip. So you can't trust everything that you hear unless you have some evidence to support it."

"Right." Mark folded his arms. "That might have made sense if I wasn't also hearing it from you."

"I'm telling you the real story of a real hero that protected The City for years on end."

"So—you don't see a problem with any of this?"

"A problem with what?"

"With everything that he's been saying."

"Life is a complicated pile of mess. We both know that."

"Uh-huh." Mark nodded. His arms tightened. "All right. Go ahead and finish your story."


"What happen after he became too popular to ignore? What did you decide to do?"

"I decided to have a talk," he replied. "I couldn't schedule a meet up because I didn't know him. I went out at night and flew around The City until I found him. It didn't take too long."

"Wait a minute. Did you just say believe half of what you see and none of what you hear?"

"I said that five minutes ago."

"I know. It just popped back in my head."

"Ok. What about it?"

"You live your life based off of that?" Mark raised his eyebrows.

"Yeah." Chaz nodded. "You could say that."

"That is the dumbest quote I have ever heard."

"What do you mean? People lie and fake things. How many times have you seen a picture that was edited? What about that anchor from KRP news who wrote a fake story about being a hostage? So how is that dumb?"

"Based off of that, how could you believe anything? Most of what you learn in life is from people telling you, and you're saying that you can't believe any of it? Not only that, but you can only believe half of what you see?"

"And?"

"What do you mean, 'and'? People are all about visuals and all of our history is basically audio."

"People that aren't blind or deaf."

"Come on Chaz. That's beside the point. Your whole conversation with Mr. Marvelous is verbal." Mark raises his hands. "Everything you tell me is verbal. Does that mean I shouldn't believe anything you've said?"

"Why are you trying to make everything so literal? It's a quote to remind you to be a skeptic and not gullible."

"Where did you find him?" I asked.

"He was at the C&M Industries building, sitting on the parapet. As soon as I landed, he knew I was there."

"What was he doing up there?"

"That's where he would go to look over The City. He told me that when I asked the same question. He said that it was the tallest building downtown, so it made things easier for him."

"I know it might be hard to remember all of these interactions from back then, but if you could give me as much information about your meeting as possible, that would be good."

"Sure. I muted my landing as much as possible." Mr. Marvelous scratched the back of his head. "I had a little bit to drink before I went to find him. But—as I said, it didn't work out, and he heard me as soon as I touched down. He didn't turn around to greet me. He asked me what I wanted. So I told him, I came to see you. I told him how I've been noticing what he was doing around The City and that I thought he was doing a good job."

"Right." Mark dipped a drumstick and stuck it in his mouth.

Chaz eyes narrowed. His upper lip began to curl, but he continued with his story.

"I said, soon you're going to need better gadgets. You're moving up to the majors, and your trinkets aren't going to cut it when you're fighting against a super villain or two. He didn't say anything. Noise from cars and the breeze filled the void."

"Did he saying anything at all? Did he even turn around?" I asked.

"Not just yet. I tried small talk, but that was getting nowhere. So I said, we should team up. That got his attention. He spun around and stood up. I couldn't see his face. All of the light from The City was obscuring him in shadow. I think I remember people saying that he liked to attack from the shadows or hide in them. Such an oxymoron." He clinched his teeth. "He still didn't say anything. I kept talking. I told him we could be a dynamic duo of sorts, and I would let him be my side kick. I even told him about all of the perks that would come with it. He finally spoke but he didn't budge at all."

"What did he say?"

"He said, you think I want to be your sidekick? Did you think I would want your perks? He was so smug." Mr. Marvelous leered at the window. "He told me that he had been watching me."

"He was watching you?"

"Yeah." He turned his gaze upon me. My heart started racing. I could only imagine how intently he looked at the villains or even Solar. "He was watching me," Mr. Marvelous shouted and thumped his chest. "As if I'm some kind of repeat offender that has some urge to get back to business as usual."

"Did he say why?"

"No. He said he didn't want anything to do with my perks or the people that I spent my time around."

"Yep. Stay clear of corruption," Mark said to himself. "A man should always stand tall for his morals."

Mr. Marvelous shook his head. "I tried to change his mind, but I couldn't get my words right. I was so infuriated." He rubbed across his lips with his thumb. "Nothing worked. He told me that he would make it on his own and then—he was gone."

"Gone? Gone, how? What do you mean?"

"He extended his cape and jumped off the side of the building." Mr. Marvelous mimicked the movement. He stood up on the chair, lifted his arms above his head, before he hopped off. "I was shocked like you. I didn't move for a couple of seconds." He drifted down to the ground. "When I did move over to the edge, I didn't see any trace of him. I honestly wasn't interested in finding him either. I was hoping whatever he tried to do, didn't work, and instead he fell to his death."

My mouth dropped open. He just wished death on somebody; in front of me. Needless to say—I didn't know what to say.

"I had a bad temper back then." He paused and looked at me with sincerity. "I would never think that way now. That is how I felt though." He walked over and sat down in the chair. "After that, I went back to my life. I thought I could wait him out. After a while he would come across some criminal that he can't handle on his own, and he would have to come crawling back. And once that happened, The City would know who was its real hero and savior."

"Your plan didn't work." He looked down at the floor. "How long did it take before you realized things weren't going to change?"

"I waited for about two years."

"Two years. That's a long time to wait for a turn of opinion. I don't think I could've held out for that long."

Mr. Marvelous didn't speak. He didn't look at me either. He sat there, with slumped shoulders, like the weight of his past was crushing him.

"I have another question. You don't have to answer it." Mr. Marvelous looked up at me. "Why do you think they were drawn to him more than you?"

"Did you really need him to answer that?" Mark said.

"How else am I supposed to get his perspective? That's what this interview is for."

"Why did they like him more?" He stood up and walked over to the windows. "Look," Mr. Marvelous said while drawing back the curtains. They flung open exposing the night sky. "What do you see?"

The docks were covered in darkness except for the lights that were scattered across the environment like stars in the sky. The sky itself was almost empty of stars. I'm sure they were there, but their light was obscured by the luminous Moon. It was as big as it has ever gotten; hanging overhead like a disco ball.

"The Moon," he continued, "brightens the night; the time of day when predators are out. It allows you to see. You can't see everything, like you could during the day, but enough to avoid being disorientated. It helps you feel safe. It lures you in with its beauty and mystery."

"So to you, Solar is like the moon? Showing up at night and saving the citizens with his light. He's in a sense—easing their tensions at the deadliest hours."

"Not at all. What else do you see?"

I looked again and again. I didn't understand what he was getting at. Was I supposed to see something else in the sky or something on the ground? I walked over to the window to get a better view; that didn't help. So instead of saying the wrong thing, I waited for him to answer.

"The street lights?" Mark said.

"Yeah."

"I was thinking that once he started to talk about the Moon."

"He was the street lights, the lamps, and spotlights that cut through the gloom of the night," Mr. Marvelous said. "He was the neon signs and office lights. I am the Moon." He opened the main window and walked out onto the balcony. I walked out with him. The stone balcony was dry as a bone. "The Moon is larger and brighter than those lights. It casts a light that covers The City as a whole. Why have those artificial lights? I thought about that during my exile." He leaned on the railing. "The Moon was man's first source of light when night came, but—the Moon has its phases. Some days it's only half as bright, and others it isn't out at all."

After he said that, it all began to make sense to me. I understood the analogy that he was making.

"This is why man created electric lights and candles," he continued. "No—their lights don't reach as far as the heavenly body that dances around the Earth. It isn't as majestic or awe-inspiring. It is dependable and measured. They're placed where they're needed, and they exude as much light as needed."

"The brightest light casts the darkest shadows," I blurted out.

He turned to me and smiled. "I also couldn't be reached. I was out of the average person's sphere. They were limited to the Earth, and I wasn't. Solar isn't—," he shook his head, "wasn't, the same. He was down there with them. He was created by them." He pointed down to the street. A figure stood on the corner under a streetlight next to a bus stop bench. "They could bask in his glow. That gave him a connection to the people that I never had. Ultimately, I couldn't compete with accessibility." He walked back into his dwelling.

I looked at the figure a bit longer, and I thought about what he said. I thought about their different interactions with the citizens. I thought about the different villains that attacked each of them, and I thought about how people talk about each of them.

"I think we should end it here. I await your return," Mr. Marvelous said.

I turned around and nodded. "I will see you then."

# CHAPTER NINE

## The Fall

Frank walked into Reed's with a smile on his face and a fanny pack strapped around his waist. As soon as he walked in, the busboy stopped what he was doing and made his way to the kitchen. No sooner than Frank got to his seat, Hazel came out of the kitchen. The sweet smell of icing followed behind her like a stray cat. The scent caught everyone's attention before they knew what was going on.

Hazel brought out an oversized cupcake with white frosting. A single blue candle was placed in the middle of it. It burned as bright as the other lights in the deli. A wax bead slowly trickled down the side of the candle.

Frank knew what was going to happen before he even arrived. Hazel has always remembered his birthday. For forty years to this very day, she has never missed it. She had even postponed her college graduation party to make sure she could be with him on his special day.

Every year Frank would wear the same thing to his celebration; a pair of crisp black slacks, a white long sleeve dress shirt with a matching belt and penny loafers, and suspenders with buttons from the previous years attached. The first button he ever got was from a six-year-old Hazel. She won the button at a spelling bee contest. It displayed the mascot of her elementary school, Larry the Lobster. All of the buttons since have filled up both sides of his suspenders. They ranged from the size of a quarter to the size of a mason jar top. She always got a kick out of seeing the lobster, and he loved that she enjoyed it.

"Hey, Frank," Hazel exclaimed. Her voice strained as it rose in pitch. Frank smiled as wide as his age would let him. Hazel placed the cupcake in front of him. She rubbed her throat with one hand. "I think I overdid it this year," she said

Frank lightly applauded her efforts. "You surprised me," he said still smiling. He leaned over to blow the candle out.

"Stop that." She playfully tapped him on the forehead. "Wait for the birthday song."

When they were both younger, Frank would have to tell her the same thing. "Wait for the birthday song." She didn't like to wait, and as soon as she saw the cake or ice cream, she would try to take a bite. She would always protest the delay, but would follow his instructions anyway.

Frank readjusted himself in the seat in preparation. Hazel started the song off. "Happy Birthday to you." Slowly the rest of the deli joined in on the birthday song. Some of them were on key, but the majority weren't. Chaz joined in with the rest of the patrons in a low voice, almost singing to himself. Public singing had never been his strong suit. He tried once at his wedding during the ceremony. He thought it would be romantic to sing his vows to his wife. She stopped him halfway through and said, "maybe you should just say the rest of it, Honey. We don't want to take up too much of everyone's time."

While everyone sung, Frank tried one last time to sneak a taste. Hazel watched him and the cupcake like a hawk. She slapped his hand like she did his forehead earlier.

He retracted his hand and laughed. "You caught me."

After the birthday song was completed, everyone clapped and cheered except for the staff. They had already went into the kitchen while all of the commotion was going on. Frank's presence was still unpleasant to them. The newer employees who hardly knew him or of him followed the rest of the staff to show their loyalty.

"Ok, Frank, you can blow out the candle," Hazel said. As long as he was happy, it didn't matter to her if the staff was participating or not.

Frank took in a deep breath and blew as hard as he could. His dentures almost flew out of his mouth from the force. Hazel clapped, and he lit up like the candle that he just blew out.

The rest of the deli went back to their own lives, everyone except Chaz. He watched as they continued their interaction. He didn't know the connection between them, but he could see it, clear as day. It was hard for him to hear the whole conversation because of where he was sitting. Hazel's voice was easier to make out since she was facing his direction. Chaz also watched her lips to help him understand every little piece of information. Frank's side of the conversation was ten times harder. He spoke softly while he ate his cupcake.

"How is it? Do you like the flavor of the frosting?"

Frank gave some exaggerated nods.

"That's good. So, how does it feel to be seventy-five?

Since the first day he saw Frank, Chaz thought he had to have been in his late eighties. He moved like every part of his body was in pain, until he sat down on that corner stool. "Must have been some years of hard living," Chaz muttered

"That's not true. You're still a spring chicken," Hazel said, placed her hand on his shoulder. She then shook her head. "Don't worry about it. I told you already; you can have whatever you want while I'm around."

Frank reached out to hug Hazel. She slid the plate to the side and hugged Frank over the counter. She rocked him from side to side as he patted on her back.

The tender moment was interrupted by her nephew, Michael. He came crashing through the kitchen's double doors. "I need to talk to you," he said subdued, barely opening his mouth.

Frank's shoulders slumped as soon as he heard Michael's voice. "I'll be back there in a little bit," Hazel said. She pulled away from Frank but continued to hold one of his hands.

"Did you make that in the kitchen?" Michael pointed at the partially eaten cupcake.

Hazel could see and feel the change in Frank's mood. She consoled him by gently caressing his wrinkled hands. Frank looked down at the counter.

"The supplies in here are for customers," Michael's voice rose. "Not for your personal pet projects."

"I said I will be back there in a bit Michael," She shouted. Most of the patrons and the staff stopped to listen to the turmoil. One woman stopped in the middle of walking out of the door. She turned around and sat down in the nearest chair to hear the gossip. Hazel took a deep breath. "Give me a few minutes," she said in a more restrained tone. "It's his birthday."

"I don't care if it's his birthday. You can't keep using my supplies as gifts. I'm not running a soup kitchen."

"I am doing what's right." She turned to face her nephew, her brow furrowed. "He has been coming—"

"I can't keep giving away free food," Michael interrupted.

"—here since he—"

"We have been riding the line for several years now." They continue to go back and forth. Neither one listening fully to the other.

"—was a little boy—"

Michael shrugged. "I don't care."

"—I will not go against my grandfather's wishes."

"I don't care. He has been coming here for years and reaping off of our hard work."

"Listen to me."

"I don't care."

"Listen to me." Hazel's voice cracked and strained. Her face was red as a Torch Lily.

Their exchange caught the attention of the rest of the deli. The cooks that were busy completing orders stopped what they were doing and walked out front to check on the uproar. Hazel looked around at all of the observers. She rubbed her throat. "Our connection with Frank goes back decades. My Grandfather," she paused, "your Great Grandfather—"

"You can stop right there. He has been getting free food from here for longer than you have been alive," Michael said. "Why?"

"I will not cut ties with this man."

"You keep repeating that, but I want to know why. Why does he deserve all of these free meals?"

Hazel opens her mouth to speak.

"Don't know why?" Michael asked. "Well, I don't know either. I've never heard a story on why Frank is so special, he has never done anything for me, but I have to keep kicking out food for him like he's some deity."

Hazel turned to check on Frank. She tried to speak again but was interrupted by Michael once more.

"We are sacrificing for someone that doesn't sacrifice anything for us. We need help. Is he going to help us?" he asked. "I don't know how long I can keep this place going; I really don't." He placed his hand on Hazel's shoulder. "I don't want to lose this place because of tradition. He needs to start helping the people that supported him over the years."

Hazel's eyes welled up. Michael pulled her in for a tight embrace. "Frank needs to contribute and become a pillar to help keep this business staying or he needs to move on."

Frank stood up from his seat, tall and proud. He reached into his fanny pack and pulled out some cash, placed it on the counter. From the corner of her eye, Hazel saw Frank walking towards the door and then heard a piercing ring of the front door's bell. Its chime hit her ear like a last call for the train departing for parts unknown.

"Let him go."

She pushed Michael off of her, grabbed up the cash that Frank left on the counter, and rushed after him.

"He can keep his money," Michael yelled. "He's not welcomed."

Hazel burst out of the deli, almost colliding with Mark as he approached the door.

"Oh. I'm sorry," Mark said with a smile. "Are you ok?" Mark asked, noticing her tears.

Hazel wiped her eyes. Her eye liner smeared down her face. "Where did he go?"

"Where did who go?" Mark looked around.

"Frank."

"Frank? The old man?"

"Yeah." She sniffed. "I have to give this back to him." She showed him a handful of crumbled up twenty dollar bills.

"Um, I think he went up that street." Mark pointed up the block.

"Thank you."

Hazel jogged up the block calling for Frank. Mark pushed open the door to the deli.

"If you see him, let me know," Michael said to the staff. "He is not to get anything else from here. Even if he is paying. He has had too many chances." He slapped the kitchen doors open as he walked through to the back.

Mark walked over to Chaz's booth and sat down. "What did I miss?"

"Frank just got banned."

"Really? I didn't know it was going to go that far."

"It's his birthday," Chaz said with a frown.

Mark gave a sympathetic nod, but his face stayed neutral.

"He could have waited for the next day."

"Sometimes you have to cut ties with people."

"It's his birthday. Besides, he has been coming here for longer than Mike has been alive."

"And?"

Chaz took in a deep breath and let out a heavy exhale.

"What do you have for me today?" Mark asked.

"We talked about his downfall among some other things."


"Welcome," Mr. Marvelous said while standing in front of a window overlooking The City. "Have a seat." He gestured to the chair on his left. I stepped towards the chair with caution. Once again, things were different and the same at the same time. Both sides of the room that held his bedroom and study were now closed off. Everything was now in the same room. His costumes and posters were encased in a lit oak cabinet in the far corner. His bed and dresser were on the opposite side of the room. In the center between the chair and couch was a clear chimney, complete with a fireplace. The room was smaller too. The width seemed to be the same, but the height of the ceiling was cut in half.

It felt really odd to me, but he acted as if nothing had changed. I didn't know if I should bring it up or not. Maybe it's just me. I have been feeling strange recently.

"Been acting strange too," Mark said.

"I was talking about me being tired," Chaz retorted.

"Right."

Mr. Marvelous spun around towards me as I sat down. "Where do you want to start?" He looked as tired as I've been feeling. His hair was disheveled, and his eyes were puffy and dull. He almost looked the exact opposite of my first meeting with him. His costume had stains all over them. It looked like it was from sweat or something like that. His glove's finger tips were black with dirt.

"He should take some of that apartment rearranging time and put it towards dry cleaning or whatever that suit needs. Why is he still wearing it anyway?"

"I'm not saying anything like that to him. He might give me more than a middle finger next time." Chaz laughed.

"We have yet to talk about what destroyed your reputation," I noted. "What do you think was the main cause for your fall from grace?"

"The time has come. I've been dreading this conversation," he said with a heavy tone. Mr. Marvelous walked over to the couch opposite of my seat and flopped down. His heavy frame sunk into the cushions as he prepared to play patient. "All of those incidents were over forty years ago, but they still hang over my head like a guillotine." He clenched his fists and shook them in the air. "I would like to say for the record—I regret everything I did." He looked over at me squarely in the eyes. "I let it all get to my head, and I crossed the line of decency a number of times. My apologies now, like then, could never suffice for the pain I inflicted upon the populous. I also haven't won back the trust that I ruined. But—in the face of those impossibilities, I still would like to give another one of my most sincere apologies to everyone that has been affected by my actions. I am truly and wholeheartedly sorry for my actions and the suffering they have caused."

"I will make sure I print that."

He gave a warm smile. The comment seemed to give him a touch of energy.

"He's really laying it on thick," Mark murmured.

"So what started this down fall? Stress? A curiosity that turned into dependency?"

"No." He paused as if he was gathering his thoughts. "It was something more simple than that. It was having too many options and being supplied with those options whenever I asked. Sometimes it came without me asking. People wanted to please me and be around me. I didn't have to say much," he added. "That was the golden age for me. My fame was at its height for a decade. I must say though, when I first appeared, I think most people didn't know what to do with me. The youngsters gravitated to me really

144

fast. I was a dream come true." He opened his arms wide. "I was a real life superhero in the flesh. It was probably the same for you."

I smiled. He was right. Mr. Marvelous wasn't some imaginary character that I could never meet or who couldn't affect me. He was real, and he really helped people. When I was growing up, I would wish that I was born back in those days, so I could see his feats in person. I dreamed of watching him battle Tempest near the docks.

"The hero that they saw wasn't only a picture in a magazine anymore or some cartoon character on the TV screen," Mr. Marvelous continued. "Most of the adults weren't the same. They didn't trust me or my intentions. I was too powerful to trust. The military was constantly trying to put limitations on where I could be or what I should be able to do. I was considered a national threat by the president. But after The Maestro, everyone sung a different tune. All of the politicians wanted to be my friend. Celebrities sought me out for photographs, and the women—the women were all over me; from married to single, young to old. I was still as naive as a schoolboy at the time, so I didn't turn down anything. That started to get me into quite a bit of trouble."

"So it's true about the women. Did you really have several women a day, or is that just legend?"

"Yes." He smiled, and then he shook his head. "I was seeing as many women that I could fit in one day." He laughed as he reminisced. "I even started a waiting list."

"What about the women? They didn't mind how you were treating them?"

"I didn't really have a waiting list. That was a joke."

"Oh." I laughed a little. I wasn't sure what to think.

"He probably did have a waiting list. I've heard stories about that," Mark said.

"People say all kinds of things about him, but did any of them actually meet him? No." Chaz snapped back. "So it's nothing but gossip and rumors until you get some evidence."

"I was getting invited to be at different events and after parties. It was maybe two years of that, and then I started drinking."

"Ok. Help me understand this timeline. Right before you fought against The Maestro, was that around the time you met Ms. Ambers?"

"Ms. Ambers was about a year before The Maestro. Our first date was the same day I fought Dynamo. She was shopping in the area for a ballroom dress or something like that. You must forgive me; it was so long ago."

"It's fine. Like I said before, please tell me as much as you can remember."

"She was in the back of a taxi. Seconds before the driver pulled off I careened by. I almost hit the car. It gave her and the driver quite a scare. She said she held her breath through the whole fight." Mr. Marvelous laughed. His feet wiggled back and forth. "It gave me pause—to see you two, titans, duke it out in the middle of the Square like an unfettered boxing match," he said with a high pitched southern drawl.

He didn't sound anything like her. That made me chuckle.

"Needless to say, Ms. Ambers was impressed by how I defeated Dynamo. She didn't like the sight of blood, but she was delighted to see that I showed some restraint in such a heated battle."

"Where did your date night take you?"

"We went to the theater and watched one of her movies, Last Ride of Otter's Ferry. It's a western."

"I've heard of it." I wanted to get back on topic, so I steered him back in the right direction. "So you and Ms. Ambers were an item for some time before The Maestro?"

"Yes."

"Where were you living at the time?"

"I had two places. One was near Glenn Wood Park and the other was right here, The Lofts. I was able to stay at Glenn Wood rent free. I bought this place once Ms. Ambers and I parted ways. I had too many memories in Glen Wood to want to stay there."

"What caused you two to part ways?"


"He cheated on her," Mark said.

"That's another one of the stories you heard?" Chaz asked.

"Same ones he probably told you."

Chaz held his tongue and clenched his teeth. Venomous thoughts tried to escape his mouth, but he redirected those thoughts back into telling the story.


"Jealousy," Mr. Marvelous said.

"You've got to give me more than that." Mr. Marvelous didn't speak, but his eyes wandered around the room. Normally, Mr. Marvelous would stare me down if he was determined to hold his tongue. I pressed forward. "Which one of you was jealous?"

"She was the jealous one."

"From all of the women?"

"No. Those women were after her."

Something wasn't adding up. I had a feeling he wasn't telling me everything. He spoke up before I could probe for more.

"You're right. I was the one that was jealous." Mr. Marvelous worked his hands together. "It's like you can read me like a book."

I smiled at that.

"She kept talking about Solar; sun up, sun down." He snickered at his accidental pun. "It would get worst when she was drunk." He closed his eyes and gave a heavy exhale. "One night we both came home drunk, and she started it up again, talking about how cute he was, and how much she wanted to meet him. I couldn't take it, and I went too far."

"Wait a minute—"

"What?"

"He hit her?" Mark said. His hands tightened on the table.

"No. I asked him that."

"Oh." Mark relaxed. "Ok."

"You hit her?"

"No." He propped himself up a little on his elbows. "God no." He laid back and looked up at the ceiling. "No, I didn't hit her. I shook her around for a bit."

"He did what?" Mark's voice could be heard through the Deli's window. Several pedestrians looked curiously through the window as they passed by, trying to find the source of the outburst.

"What does that mean?"

Mr. Marvelous turned to look at me. "That's all I did. I promise."

Mark's eyes darted back and forth as he rubbed his head with both of his hands. "They said it was a horseback riding accident."

"Who said that?"

"The studio's Director of Public Relations said that she fell off of a horse during a filming that resulted in her shoulder being dislocated. She also had several torn muscles in the same area."

"I didn't know that."

"Her career was over because of that," Mark said through his teeth.

"I shook her a couple of times," Mr. Marvelous continued. "But since I was drunk, I used too much force. She passed out immediately."

"Did you take her to the hospital?"

"I did, but it took a while. You have to understand that we were both really drunk. I thought she passed out. I managed to take her to the bedroom without stumbling into any of the furniture." He placed a hand over his eyes. "I didn't notice her shoulder until I started undressing her. I didn't know what to do. I could see something was wrong, but I didn't know how to fix it. At that moment I thought about taking her to the hospital, but then I thought about how it would look. I needed to sober up first and come up with a plan."

Both of Mark's legs began to shake. He rubbed his hands together vigorously as he looked around the deli. The place was still busy from earlier, and the waitresses were buzzing around each table like bees on spring flowers. Chaz could see that the story was upsetting him, but he kept going. The quicker he got past this part in the story, the better.

"How long did it take?"

"It was the longest hour of my life. I was thinking about all of the headlines in the papers and tabloids that would be flying off of the stands for the next couple of months. So I called up the studio and told them that she fell down while getting off of the elevator. They told me not to take her to the main hospital until her arm is reset."

"The studio told you not to take her to the hospital? Who did they send to set her shoulder?"

"They sent one of the stunt coordinators to help with her shoulder. It was really late by the time they rang him. He had to sneak out the house so that his wife wouldn't find out. After that, we took her to the hospital to have her arm examined."

"Did you two last longer than that?"

"That was it. After that day, she didn't contact me or come back for her belongings." Mr. Marvelous covered his face with his hand. "I stayed there for a couple of weeks, but everything reminded me of her. I don't think the apartment management wanted me around after that."

"That's when you moved to this place?"

"Yes. I helped them finish off the rest of the building. With the money that I paid and the work that I did, the owner gave me my own section to use how I saw fit. I took over the whole floor so I could have privacy. I didn't want people poking about in my business."

"Do you think you should have been forgiven?"

"I would like to have been forgiven. Should she have? I can't say. I was drunk at the time, but that isn't a good excuse."


"And then him and his friends covered it up," Mark declared.

"Yeah."

Mark looked up at Chaz, upper lip twitching. "Just—yeah?"

"What else do you want me to say?"

Mark shook his head and looked out the window. "Nothing."

"I moved on. I struggled at first, but within a month I became the bachelor that every woman wanted. I was not only famous, but I was one of a kind."

"After Ms. Ambers, did you start drinking more frequently?"

"Yes I did. I became more open to everything. A broken heart looks for anything to fill its cracks."

"What was your first drink?"

"It was some kind of rum—maybe not." He shrugged. "I'm sorry, I forgot the name of the drink. I didn't know my drinks back then. People would hand it to me, and I would gulp it down. That one in particular was given to me by Ms. Ambers. Do you drink?" He reflected the question back on me.

"I used to drink a lot back in college." I chuckled. "I had way too much to drink at a party, and I was dared to do a back flip off of a coffee table."

Mr. Marvelous laughed. He sounded like a child laughing in his school's play. It was loud, boastful, and fake. I looked at him, and he stopped abruptly. Maybe, he thought he was out of place by finding my story funny.

"I didn't stick the landing and crashed through the table. I cracked a couple of ribs and almost punctured my lung with one of the wood pieces." I almost fell apart. I kept eye contact with him as long as I could. I felt a smile coming, so I turned and looked out the window. "I went straight to the hospital that night. The doctor said I was lucky. If the piece of wood was any sharper, I might not have made it. So since that day, I haven't wanted to test my luck."

I turned back around to him staring at me with a blank face. The kind of face that poker champions dream of. Once again I attempted to up the ante. "Do you want to see the scar?" He kept staring at me for what seemed like ten minutes. But I guess he could already see through my story.

He gave me smirk. "Nice try. Almost convincing. Next time pick an incident that you actually saw, that might have worked out better. No," he wagged his finger, "You have never tried anything like that in your life."


"Why are you lying in the first place?" Mark said.

"I don't know." Chaz shrugged. "I wanted to see if I could."

"And all it did was backfire."

"I was just having a little bit of fun."

"Having fun by lying to the person you're interviewing? What happened to setting an example?"

"Setting an example? You say that like he's some child. I don't see a problem with it, and he didn't either. He laughed about it."


"You're right. That happened to my friend..."

"Oscar."

"Yeah. How did you..." He never told me. Honestly, I wasn't sure if I should push the matter. I mean, I am there to interview him. I wasn't there to go through my life.

"I tried whatever they put in front of my face." He licked his lips.

"Did the drugs follow that? That includes snorting, smoking, or pills."

He nodded his head. I think those were implied, but I felt like I still needed to ask. I needed an overview of it, nothing too specific. The next question would be the heavy hitter.

"Who did you get the drugs from? Being as though you're Mr. Marvelous, the savior of The City, everyone would have known who you were. Not to mention the blowback if people found out that a superhero who's supposed to be fighting crime is buying drugs from a neighborhood dealer."

"That would have caused quite a stir. But it would have been more on the side of class then illegal substances. Everyone in that circle was using something. It was de facto legal for us."

"What do you mean?"

"If any kind of investigation would have happened, all of the public officials would have been locked up. And after they went away, you would have to go after over half of the police department, judges and lawyers."

That was shocking to hear. You know? Over the years, you would hear the rumors about different politicians but all of them, and the source isn't some random informant looking for a quick payout either. It was coming from the mouth of Mr. Marvelous himself. Then, the fact that more than half of the law enforcement was dirty too; my mind was completely blown.

"The first person to introduce me to coke and prostitutes was Malone Bell."

"Malone Bell? That name sounds familiar." I gave myself some time to ponder the name. "Malone...Mayor Malone?"

He nodded.

"But he was the 'say nope to dope' Mayor. How many people knew he was using drugs?"

"Nobody in his staff."

"Wait. Before you got into it, why didn't you shut the whole situation down? Did you ever look back at that time and think, what if?"

"I wasn't told that the women were street walkers until after I already had sex with a couple of them. By that time it was too late. The drugs came after all of the drinking and women. As far as looking back on life and wondering what if; well—that was decades ago. I'm over that now. I came up with a new way to atone. That's why you're here."

He was right. Nothing could change what he did, especially not wishing for a do-over. Time flows one way, forward. The only option he had was to except his choices, and he has been doing that for these past four decades. I remember sitting there thinking about how much pressure had been placed on him throughout those years. Could I continue to stand with all of that weight? Even with all of his abilities, I don't think I would have lasted one year in his position.

"His position?"

"Yeah," Chaz said. "He had to constantly save The City and its inhabitants from peril. He was expected to do that, day in and day out, perfectly. I can't even wash dishes without breaking one from time to time. I think that is why I was never surprised or upset when I heard about some of the destruction that happened while he was fighting the villains."

"I'm sure it was hard job, but that's what comes with being a savior. Other people can deal with it in their jobs, and you could too."

"It's not the same. He had more on the line."

"Ok. He had more on his plate because it was a bigger job. I can agree with that. But like I said before, it can be done. We have an example of that already."

"What example? Police? They didn't have to go against villains like The Maestro."

Mark shook his head. His nose flared ever so slightly as he exhaled. "I'm not talking about any of his rogues gallery or the police."

"Then who?"

"Solar."

Chaz opened his mouth for a quick rebuttal but stopped short of actually speaking. He scratched his head as he pondered. "That's only one person. If it was that easy, more people would have been doing it."

Mark cocked his head to the side. "Really? That's all you got?"

"Yeah," Chaz said with confidence.

"Fine. Just get back to the story."


Like I said, I was thinking—were all of the drugs and drinking nothing but a form of escapism? A way to relieve some of his built up stresses. Right before I got a chance to ask the next question, Mr. Marvelous answered it.

He sat up on the couch; swinging his legs around and planting them firmly on the ground. "I've never tried to escape from anything in my life." His lips tightened. "Never," Mr. Marvelous said, "Understand?"

His outburst shocked me. I nodded in agreement.

He sprang to his feet, cuffing his hands around his back. His demeanor went back to what I was used to seeing, calm and relaxed. "I saw something new, and I wanted to be a part of it. They were nice to me. It was always an inviting, warm feeling I would get from all of them."

"If it wasn't escapism, what were you doing?"

"I was living life. I wasn't doing my nightly patrols at all. I couldn't do both at the same time. Having a good time was more important. "

I rapped my fingers on the edge of the arm rest. "That's around the time Solar showed up and the crime rate increased."

"Yeah. Crime soared like the Pelican." He laughed to himself. "Some of the reporters and citizens that held out with accepting me were now going after my reputation. Believe it or not, it had a tremendous effect on me; much more than most people would think. My esteem was as weak as any other man. I acted like a child. I doubled down on my vices instead of listening to the criticisms. I used more drugs and chased more women. Super villains like Sergeant Terror were still showing up to attack The City, and I would still battle them, but sometimes I would get to the incidents too late. Some of the destruction could have been avoided if I would have dispensed the threat in a timely fashion."

I leaned forward in the seat, slid closer to the edge. "You said Sergeant Terror? I remember hearing about him. He is the one that stole a bunch of military armaments and tried to wipe out Congress for them cutting the Defense budget."

He paced back and forth while he spoke. "We were at peace for more than a decade. He said it was a necessity for our country to stay vigilant at all times and if our government couldn't see that then it was time for them to be replaced. I followed his tracks to his hideout deep in Arbrey County's forest. Half of the forest was booby trapped. I have never been more annoyed fighting a villain in my life." He laughed and then cleared his throat. "He snuck out while I was making my way inside his cabin."

"How long did it take you to realize he was gone?"

"I figured it out when the cabin exploded with me in it," he replied. "The blast ejected me from the building. It stung for a brief moment, but it wasn't enough to truly injure me. If I was a normal man, I would have died easily." Mr. Marvelous wiped his arms and legs. "I dusted myself off, got my bearings, and then chased after him. I found him five minutes outside of The City on Route 322. Luckily there was an accident on the road. If not, he would have made it into The City before I could reach him."

"What happened once you caught up with him?"

"He brought everything he had left with him in a 6X6 truck. The motorist were like sitting ducks. Sergeant Terror was willing to attack whomever, just to make his point. It took me several minutes to get past all of his missiles, bullets, and flames while still protecting everyone who was stuck on the road. All the drinking the day before didn't help either. My head was spinning the whole time." He hung his head. "That was a normal occurrence though. I had a hangover every morning around that time."

"Every morning?"

"Or I would sleep in. Noon was always a good time to wake up."

"You didn't see a problem with that?

Of course, now I do, but at the time..." he shrugged. "No one complained."

"Not a single person? What about public opinion, had it not changed by then?"

Mr. Marvelous raised his head and nodded. "People always talk, but they often don't say it to whomever that really needs to hear it," He looked dejected, as if he knew where the conversation was headed, wanting to change its course but knowing that all of it was inevitable. "I wouldn't have listened anyway..."

"Because you were Mr. Marvelous."

He looked down at the floor. "I was used to people either doing what I wanted, or using force to get what I wanted. Those actions—at times, spilled over in to the lives of regular civilians."

"What happened?"

Mr. Marvelous scratched the back of his head. "I smacked around a couple of girls."


"You see," Mark blurted out.

Chaz continued with the story.


My heart sank down to my stomach.

"The hits weren't enough to send them to the hospital. I only hit them hard enough to make my point." Mr. Marvelous walked back over and sat down on the couch defeated. "I know that doesn't make it any better." His upper body slumped over onto his legs. He stared at the floor as he recounted what happened. "The first one or two incidents were hidden from the public like with Ms. Ambers. I would pay them off or give them some kind of gift to get back into their good graces, but for some of the women, that wasn't enough. We couldn't keep them all quiet."

"Who is the 'we' that you speak of?"

"Yeah, who's that?" Mark echoed.

"They were some of my acquaintances from the parties." Mr. Marvelous looked up with a frown. I didn't think he would want me to pursue the question any further, so I stayed quiet. "Some of the women told stories to reporters of physical violence and unwanted sexual advancements," he continued. "I don't think I did any of the sexual advancements, but I was extremely drunk most of the time. It was all in the papers."

I nodded. "But why? What was happening between you and those women that caused so many assaults?"

"I don't know. I really don't." Mr. Marvelous stretched his neck by pulling it to each side. He then rotated his shoulders. It looked like he was trying to knock the weight of guilt off of him. "All of that was lumped together with the destruction of property I would cause on my nights out on the town. One day the officials gathered together and voted for me to be exiled."

"Who were the people that voted?"

"Mayor Malone, Governor Nick Woods, some of the celebrities I was partying with, both senators: Charles Peters and Sasha Ingram, and Carlos Dover."

"What was the count?"

"Not a single vote against. They all turned their backs on me."

Rejection at the highest degree. He kept their secrets, drank, and did drugs with them on an almost daily basis, and they still had a meeting behind his back to exile him from the community.

"It would have worked," he continued, "but at that time they still needed me. I was their drug. They would try to stay strong and put me off to the side, but after a while, they would come right back."

I refrained from interrupting his thought with another question. I could see that his mind was still churning and something was bubbling up, but I didn't think it was going to go in the direction that it did.

"Please save us," he mocked, "You have to stop him." He shook his head, one hand balled up tight in the other. "Right after I saved them from being consumed by the next villain, I was casted off to the side. It was a tug-of-war." His heel tapped rapidly on the floor like a woodpecker. His arm on the same side vibrated from the motion. "With Solar being there, people didn't need me as much. He would show up right in the nick of time with all of his fancy gadgets. They were toys really. He wasn't as capable as me, but he was always there." He nodded. "He didn't expect anything in return, and he didn't accept anything either. I found that out first hand when I approached him that night on the roof."

His voice switched from angry tones to more of a sorrowful sound. All of his feelings from the past were raging back again.

"I was a collapsing star," he continued, "that got too big too fast, and through that expansion I exploded." His head hung low as he spoke. "Solar gained enough skill to survive in the big leagues, and the villains weren't as deadly as before. So, I wasn't needed anymore. All of people, and the parties, and the free gifts started to disappear. Even people I saved from death, not only knocking at their door but ripping it off its hinges, they left me too. After that, I was left alone to my own devices; which was a large sum of money and a habit I couldn't kick. I wasn't getting the drugs and drink for free anymore, but I still had a need for it, more than ever. It took three months to run through the last bit of my money, and four months for the last public appearance."

"So you started drinking early in your career with Ms. Ambers. After you two split, you began to drink more and experiment with drugs. How long was it before you were over your head?

Mr. Marvelous hopped back to his feet. "It only took one day and then I was hooked." He placed his finger in the corner of his mouth like a fish on the line. "Sex, booze, and drugs; the life of a hero." He wiped the saliva from his finger onto his pants. "They were the shackles that controlled me and the vices that Solar stayed clear of. It went from a luxury that might happen twice a day, to a standard that I demanded wherever I went." He walked over to the windows. "That might have been it." He placed his hands on the glass doors. The sunlight beamed in his face. He closed his eyes, basking in the intensity. "I had a temper back then, and I didn't like when people said no to me."


"The drugs and drinks were happening so often that it became like water at a restaurant." Chaz lifted his empty cup. "Some people want it, and some people never even touch the glass, but that doesn't stop those same people from being bewildered by its absence."

Mark looked down at his cup. It had been sitting in the same place since the waiter brought it over, filled up to the brim. "Is that what he said, or are you making a guess?"

"All I'm doing is letting you know what I heard. That's why he started getting wild towards the end. I mean, other than the incident with Ms. Ambers. After being catered to for so long, he wasn't used to the real world anymore. Those habits didn't crossover once he was forced out of that bubble."

"I need to live in that bubble. How are you going to have all of that thrown at you and then you blow it? He's a dumb-ass. Did you tell him that?"

"I asked him about it."

"No—did you tell him he was a dumb-ass? Because that's what he is. How the fuck? Does he even know how hard it is for everyone else? This fucking guy. Now I'm supposed to feel sorry for this fucker?"

"He can't go through stress like everyone else? Nobody is perfect."

"Stress from what?" Mark scoffed at the idea. "You were right at first. I will give you that. Neither one of us were born when he was saving The City, and so everything I heard about him was from second hand stories. I knew hearing him out was important to you, so I thought I should give him a chance. But guess what—all those stories are true. People said he was a womanizer, and they were right."

"Yeah. People make mistakes."

"Mistakes," Mark roared. His eyes were on fire. "Running a stop sign is a mistake. Spilling a drink at a party is a mistake. Drug chasing and slapping around women isn't a fucking mistake; that's a decision."

"I get it. It happened. He isn't denying it. He's trying to tell his side of the story."

"I can tell it for him. One day he gets his special abilities and shoots to fortune and fame without doing shit. Then he pisses it all away because he didn't know how to handle it. Bullshit." Mark jammed his finger into the table. "Everything is dropped in his lap, and he wants to complain about it. Well I know what his problem is—he didn't have to work for it."

"When he fought with... "

"Uh-uh. Don't even bring that up." Mark waved his hands back and forth. "From what you said, he never had a hard time with any of it. Everybody loves an underdog right? Isn't that what he said?" Mark steamrolled through any possible retort that Chaz might have had. "He's been faking it the whole time. This mother fucker..." Some spittle sprayed from Mark's mouth as he gnashed his teeth. He wiped his mouth with the back of his hand. "Now he is trying to blame everyone else. And what are they going to say about it? They aren't going to say shit because all of them are dead."

"But— "

"They're fucking dead, Chaz. He could tell you anything—and then he is back to being the underdog. Are you fucking kidding me? Fuck that guy, Chaz. Fuck 'em. He got what he got because of himself. Nothing more, nothing less."

"All right. Chill out." Chaz looked around Reed's. Their argument has caught the attention of some of the patrons. "You are making too much noise," he said in a hushed tone. "Look—I get it. You would have loved to be in his position. And I know you have lived a hard life, but you don't know how hard it was for him. The grass is always greener on the other side."

Mark lowered his voice but not nearly as much as Chaz would have liked him to. "Fuck all that. If it was somebody else I might understand. But we aren't talking about someone else. We are talking about Mr. Marvelous. I've been a hard worker all of my life, and whatever you get you earn it. I learned that from my parents. But now you're telling me that this guy's fucking life was hard because he got too much free shit. And not only that, you're on his side?"

"I never said I was on his side. It's not about sides anyway."

"Really?"

"I can understand where he is coming from. I don't think I would have made the same choices, but I can see why he made them, and that's all that he wants. He wants people to hear both sides of the story so they can see why he chose the paths that he did."

"Right." Mark crossed his arms, resting them on top of the table. "So you're against everything he's done?"

"I don't think I would have done that stuff, but I can't do the things he can do."

"It's a simple question Chaz," he said, putting emphasis on every word. "Would you rob a bank or stab someone?"

Chaz shook his head. "No."

"See, it's that simple. A yes or no. Are you against what Mr. Fucking Marvelous has done?"

"Well—"

"Stop acting like a politician. Yes or fucking no."

"Yes. I'm against it. But—"

"Then why are you trying to defend it?"

"I'm not. I am just trying to make you see it from his perspective."

"No, you're defending it. That fuck face got you blinded. That's probably why he wore the suit and showed you all of the memorabilia." Mark nodded with a grimace. "Yep. That guy is playing you."

"No." Chaz shook his head in disbelief. "He doesn't want a fluff piece. He wants an unbiased story about his life and what he went through during and after his stint as a hero. That's it."

"Right. Keep believing that shit. I don't know what to tell you." Mark looked back down at his cup. Water droplets slid down the side to a ring of water around its base. "That mother fucker...Every time I think about it."

"Can I finish the story?"

"I don't want to hear anymore. I'm getting hot as shit right now. I don't know how you can do it. Matter of fact, call me after you're done with all of this."

# CHAPTER TEN

## Last day

Chaz was face down in his bed; one arm hung off the side, grazing the carpet. The house's silence was interrupted by his periodic heavy breathing. He mimicked a hibernating bear; growling in its sleep to persuade scavengers from sneaking into its cave. He was fully dressed from the day before. Even his Oxfords were still on.

The room was practically empty. No dressers, nightstands, head board, or mirrors; there were only the bed and three large plastic bins filled with clothes and shoes. The comforter and sheets were all on the floor in a pile next to the bins. The one pillow that was left on the bed was perched on his head, hiding his face from the morning light.

"Welcome." The voice woke Chaz up from his deep sleep. He sprang to life, rolling himself off of the side of the bed, landing on his hands and knees. He roared with half open eyelids as he flexed his body. The arm that previously dangled off the edge tingled with pins of needles. He shook it to speed up the blood flow to his numb fingertips. The room was muggy. His brow and shirt were both damp with sweat.

Chaz sat up, wiping the sleep from his eyes. He heard his phone chime downstairs. Sluggish, he made his way downstairs, cautious with each step, he stopped on the last step. He checked in the living room. Two plants out of the many that occupied the living room were wilting and browning from neglect. The television was unplugged and leaning against the fireplace. Pieces of packages and dirt were swept into a small pile in the center of the room. The walls in the hallway were mostly empty, except for a portrait of Chaz and Tracy right before their move back to The City, and a large, oval, wall-mounted mirror that hung in a landscape fashion.

Chaz rubbed his eyes as he walked into the kitchen in search of his phone. As he approached, the phone grew louder, the sound bounced around in his head like an echo chamber. His head pounded from the sound. The room smelled of fresh paint. Most of the surfaces were covered with old canvas tarps. The kitchen had been painted a pea green, but the color made Tracy sick. She couldn't eat in there without feeling nauseous. Repainting it was on the top of her list for home improvements. They decided—she decided and Chaz just agreed, to have ivory cabinets, pale blue pastel walls, and gray hardwood tile on the floor. Most of the room had been painted so far. An empty paint bucket sat open with a dried up roller hanging out of it.

The phone vibrated on the table with each ring. It creep towards the edge of the table, stopping just before its event horizon. He picked up the phone on the last ring, not bothering to check the caller ID. "Hello." There was silence on the other end followed by two clicks. Chaz sat down in the closest chair. "Hello," he repeated. The phone clicked two more times. He checked to see if the call was dropped. It was still connected, but he didn't recognize the number.

A faint voice called for him. "Chaz."

He put the phone back to his ear. "Hello. Who is this?" The person spoke again, but he couldn't make out what they were saying. The person sounded muffled, and their words were disjointed. "Can you say that again? You're breaking up."

"Chaz, it's Mark."

"Hey."

"Where are you?"

"I'm in the house. I just woke up about ten minutes ago." Chaz yawned.

"Sleeping in again? I wish I could do that. I've been up and at a job since 5:30."

Chaz wiped his face with his free hand. "Yeah."

"Are we still meeting today?"

"Today's my last day. You still want to meet up?"

"Last day? How? You just started last week. Did you find something better?"

"No. The interview." Chaz cleared his throat. "I was going to wait a couple more days. I should be finished with the article by then."

"Damn. I was looking forward to catching up. Why didn't you tell me you wanted to change the days?"

"I know, but you were so pissed off last time. I'm doing what you asked."

"What are you talking about? You've got to be thinking of someone else. Did you save my number in your phone?"

"I saved it the same day you gave it to me."

"What number do you have?"

Chaz checks the phone and tells him the number he sees and then questions him about the area code.

"That's the right number. I didn't say anything like that."

"You told me two days ago at Reed's."

"Like I said, you've got to be talking about someone else. I was working Monday, and I haven't been to Reed's in years. I was only going there today because you suggested it. I'd rather go to a bar or something."

"Stop playing around. I'm tired."

"Why would I be playing?"

A humming sound in Chaz's ears grew with intensity in the silence between each exchange. The sound started off low like the sound of power going through a television. By the last question, the sound became almost deafening, drowning out the rest of what Mark was saying. "Do you hear that? I think I'm having a signal problem. Hold on." He examined the phone, checking the antenna strength, and the volume. Nothing seemed out of the ordinary. "Hello?" The phone fell silent as the house that he was in, then two clicks. "Mark, are you still there?" Chaz checked the phone again to see if the call dropped.

# MAGNANIMOUS ABSOLUTION

A low voice came from the direction of his living room, "Have a seat." Chaz's head spun to see who spoke.

The voice woke Chaz up from his deep sleep. Hours old saliva left a trail on his face from his mouth, down past his chin. He sprang to life, rolled over to his back, and stretched all of his appendages out like a starfish. He roared with half open eyelids. The room was muggy. His brow and shirt were both damp with sweat. His tie hung loose around his neck.

He sat up, wiping the sleep from his eyes. He heard his phone chime downstairs. He drew the blinds and opened the bedroom window. The autumn wind blew in as cold as a winter's breeze. It chilled him in an instant.

Still groggy, Chaz shuffled down the stairs, cautious with each step. He had fell down the stairs more than once already. The last time, two days ago, he descended the stairs too fast in his socks. He managed to make it safely down more than halfway before slipping and crashing into the volute. The collision loosened it and bruised two of his ribs. Since that day, both Chaz and Tracy not only took their time but also held onto the banister if they weren't wearing shoes.

Their home was almost complete. An assortment of small potted plants, a couch, and television decorated the living room. Their old loveseat was still covered in stretch wrap. In the hallway hung pictures of each side of their immediate family. Chaz and Tracy had their own designated side for their pictures.

Chaz rubbed his eyes as he walked into the kitchen in search of his phone. The room smelled of basil, garlic, and oils from last night's dinner. Pots and pans hung from a rack over top of the island. The counter was covered with plastic grocery bags. His phone was on the kitchen table next to an open moving box, kitchen, written on its side.

The phone vibrated on the table with each ring. It crept towards the edge of the table, stopping just before its event horizon. Tracy walked into the kitchen after him. "Your phone keeps ringing." She walked over to the box and pulled out a food processor. It was wrapped with pieces of newspaper.

Chaz's eyes widened once he saw her. There she was, the love of his life, carrying on as if nothing happened a few days prior. She looked as beautiful as ever. Black shiny heels raised her height higher than normal. She was now only two inches shorter than him. He stared at her with the same passion and wonder that he had the first time he laid eyes on her.

"What?" She placed the food processor down on the table. "Something wrong?"

"No." He took a few steps closer, grinning like he won a prize. "It's just good to see you."

She smiled, barely showing any teeth.

"I need to say something." Chaz stepped closer.

"Oh yeah?" She blushed.

"Yeah. It's about the other day." He grabbed Tracy by the hand and kissed it. She smelled of lavender. "I know I said somethings —" His phone rang again. It buzzed around on the table, grabbing both of their attention.

"You should probably answer that. It might be important."

"Ok." Chaz sat down in the closest chair. "I still need to talk to you."

"I'm not going anywhere." She leaned over and kissed him on the lips, soft and gentle. "Cross my heart." She motioned a cross over her cleavage. He watched her switch out of the kitchen. Her hips swayed like a pendulum. He was hypnotized.

He picked up the phone on the last ring, not bothering to check the caller ID. "Hello?" There was silence on the other end followed by two clicks. His brow collapsed together. "Hello," he repeated. The phone clicked two more times. He checked to see if the call was dropped. It was still connected, but he didn't recognize the number.

A faint voice called out for him. "Chaz."

He put the phone back to his ear. "Yeaaahh..." The person spoke again but he couldn't make out what they were saying. Their voice was muffled and their words were disjointed. "You're breaking—"

"Hold on. I'm near a bunch of trees."

The voice sounded familiar. "Tracy?"

"Yes," the voice on the other end replied.

Chaz laughed. "Stop playing on the phone."

"Playing on your phone? Look, my mother said you kept calling the house."

Tracy walked back into the kitchen. Her heels clacked on the floor with each step. "Yes?"

Chaz's heart sped up. He shook his head at her with wide eyes.

She looked on with concern. "Is everything ok?" Both the voice and Tracy said in unison. He froze in place, slack-jawed.

"Chaz," they continued to echo one another. "Are you alright?"

His body shook with adrenaline.

"What's wrong?"

Chaz forced the words out of his mouth. "Where are you?"

"I thought you wanted to talk."

"I do..."

"So..." Tracy walked closer to Chaz. He recoiled. "Where do you want to start?"

Chaz woke up from a deep sleep, staring up at the ceiling fan. It wobbled as it spun. His brow and shirt were both drenched with sweat. Most of the air from the mattress had escaped throughout the night. Sunlight beamed through the naked window, heating up the room. The air was thick and muggy.

Chaz sat up, wiping his face with his sleeve. He tried to piece together what happened, but the details faded with every passing second. "Just a dream," he sighed, scratching his head. The bright sun that heated him up in his sleep was deceiving. When he opened the window, nothing but cool air crept in through the opening and spilled toward the ground like a fog from a refrigerator. The air chilled his naked feet. He stretched, stripped of his clothes, and hopped in the shower.

His phone chimed downstairs. He threw on some clothes and made his way downstairs, cautious with each step, he stopped at the bottom. Jackets and coats were draped over the volutes on each of the banisters. The place was relatively empty. All of the plants that had filled up the majority of space in the living room were now gone. The couch, TV, and most of the pictures were gone too. Trash and dirt had been swept up into a pile in the center of the room. The love seat that Tracy asked him to throw out was still there, more ragged than ever. A few boxes covered one side of the seat. The walls in the hallway were naked with exposed tan lines from the missing picture frames and mirrors.

Chaz rubbed his eyes as he walked into the kitchen in search of his phone. As soon as he crossed the threshold, he could feel a headache coming on. The pain started right above his eyes on either side. Week old pizza boxes and food containers were stacked, lopsided, on the island's counter. The room smelled stale. Both sinks were filled with dirty dishes. Flies patrolled the sinks, occasionally landing to eat or clean themselves. The granite counter-tops were also unkempt and covered with food particles and used pots. "I'll clean them when I get back."

The phone vibrated on the table with each ring. It crept toward the edge of the table, stopping just before tipping off the edge. He picked up the phone and checked the caller ID. He didn't recognize the number, but he answered anyway. "Hello." There was silence on the other end followed by two clicks. Chaz sat down in the closest chair. "Hello," he repeated. The phone clicked two more times. He hung up immediately and placed it back on the table. The whole situation felt so uncomfortably familiar.

Chaz flipped the phone over, his feet tapped the ground, his palms grew sticky with sweat. He got up and paced in front of the table. "It's just déjà vu That's it. Déjà vu," he muttered. He picked up the phone and called back the number. He continued to pace while it rang.

Carlos, the paper's intern, answered the call. He had been working at the paper for six months as a gofer; mainly used to 'go for' copies, food, and anything else the staff needed at the time. Chaz was relieved. "Hey, Carlos. Can you get Bernard for me?"

"Chaz?" He whispered back. "Where are you?"

"I'm home." He cleared his throat. "Why are you whispering?"

"Home?"

"Yeah. Stop asking so many questions. Go get Bernard."

"He's busy right now. There's a staff meeting going on. I'm right next to the door."

"Someone called me from this number. Do you know who?"

"No. I've been on the move all day."

Chaz could faintly hear some talking on Carlos's side of the line. "Chaz. Yeah, he just called," Carlos said to the person or persons in the background.

"What's going on?" Ringing in his ear resonated through his head. The space between his brain and skull shrank. It felt like his brain was trying to escape.

"Ok. I will tell him. Chaz? Are you still there?"

"Yeah. I'm here." The noise got strong with the pain.

"Drew wants you to come in." Drew is the metro assistant section editor. His first day at the paper was three years before Chaz. Outside of the job, he treated Chaz like his little brother.

"I can't." He rubbed around the back of his free ear. "I have to...just put Drew on the phone."

"Hold on Chaz," Carlos said. "Yeah. He's at home." The background voice was still muffled, but he could hear that it became agitated. "He said he will call you after the meeting."

"Wait..." The throbbing pain flowed down the back of his neck. Sweat beaded on his forehead. His eyes grew sensitive to even the minimum light that lit up the kitchen.

"Got to go. Bye," Carlos said before he hung up.

Chaz pushed a heavy exhale out through his mouth like a child with a birthday wish. The floor wobbled beneath his feet. He stumbled to the table and collapsed onto the nearest chair. Both, he and the chair, hit the ground with a thud. His face bounced from the impact.

His eyes opened, head throbbed, and his stomach churned. He was sprawled out on the loveseat, feet hung off the side, phone in hand by his ear.

"Are you still there?"

"Yeah..." Chaz rubbed his face.

"Good. Bernard and I came to the same decision," Drew said. "The interview is taking too long. You said two weeks. It's been more than three months now."

Chaz sat up in the seat. His back was hurting as bad as his head.

"We need the article before the end of the week. That gives you three more days," Drew said. "I'm sorry," his voice softened. "I get it. You just moved here, everything is new, and then you're hit with a huge story. A huge story you didn't have to take by the way, but you did, and I applaud the gumption. Doing that takes a lot of courage, but just having courage doesn't get you the award. You have to follow through. When you take on something like that, it's a career making or ending moment. Look, I took a huge risk with you and this story. Do you understand what I am saying?"

"Yeah."

"I'm going to be one hundred percent with you, ok? Completely Frank—this is not looking good Chaz. Not at all. I hope you prove us wrong."

"I will get it done Drew. Today is the last day. I swear, you can count on me."

"We will see." Drew hung up.

Chaz pinched the bridge of his nose and sighed. The pain had finally started to subside. A cool sensation washed over his head from his brow to the base of his skull. He got up and rushed upstairs to finish getting dressed.

He walked out of the house in a thin trench coat. In his haste, he missed the last two stairs and stumbled. He looked around to see if anyone had noticed his blunder. Three teenagers were gathered on the steps of his neighbor's house holding court. The group whispered to each other as they looked over in his direction. He couldn't really make out what they were saying, but he could tell that they were talking about him.

"Hello," he said with a smile, trying to be polite. They continued to talk amongst themselves, never acknowledging his greeting. "What's that smell?" Chaz pondered. He stopped in his tracks, looking around the neighborhood for the origin of the scent. All of a sudden, Chaz's vision blurred. The sound from the passing car, chirping birds, and all of the other ambient noises became muffled and distant. The world became points of fuzzy light.

A car honked two houses up. It brought the world back into focus. He stood outside of his gate facing his front door, his hand lifting its latch. It was still wet from the day before, while everything else looked free of that moisture. Chaz looked around and sniffed the cold air. The scent he noticed earlier was now gone, replaced by the smell of exhaust.

Two more honks from the same car drew him to it. Chaz closed the latch on the gate and wiped off his hands with a napkin he had in his coat pocket. He zipped to the cab and hopped in. "Take me to the docks."

# CHAPTER ELEVEN

## Last day Part II

Chaz opened the door to Mr. Marvelous' home. The wood floor creaked and shifted as he moved through the entry. Mr. Marvelous stood in front of the windows. All of the shades were drawn except for the one in front of him. His arms crossed behind his back, one holding on to the other by the wrist.

"Welcome," Mr. Marvelous said as he did every time Chaz has arrived. "Where do you want—"

By the time he spoke those words, Chaz had already sat down in the chair. His hands tapped rhythmically on the top of his thighs. Mr. Marvelous turned around, his head cocked to one side. His lips perked up to speak. Chaz's head rocked as he stared at the chair across from him.

Mr. Marvelous strolled over to the chair. He peered at Chaz with furrowed eyebrows. "Straight to business today?"

"Yeah." He looked up. "I'm sorry." He rubbed his eyes. "I'm going through some things."

"Let me guess—" His lips peeled back exposing his teeth. "—your wife."

"I never told you I was married," Chaz said sharply.

Mr. Marvelous didn't speak. He pointed to Chaz's hand. His wedding band wasn't there, but the evidence was; a ring of pale skin encompassed his finger. Chaz shook his head. "Is it because of me, or does she think you're cheating again?"

Chaz started to question, but he changed his mind at mid thought. "It's complicated." He looked down as he hunched over in the seat. "You could say it's a little of both."

"And I did," Mr. Marvelous said with a smirk.

Chaz brushed the comment off. "It has to do with my childhood friend too. But I—I don't want to talk about it."

"You don't trust me?" Mr. Marvelous walked to his side.

He shook his head. "It's not that. I just want to finish this up so my life can go back to normal." Chaz looked up at Mr. Marvelous. "I didn't mean any disrespect. Things have been getting rough since this whole thing started."

"Today will be the last day," he patted Chaz on the shoulder. Chaz's muscles tightened from the unexpected touch. "After that—I'd like to pay you back."

"Your story is enough."

"Wait for the end."

Chaz nodded. "Ok."

Mr. Marvelous patted him one last time and then walked back over to his chair. His hand was heavy. "Now—" He took a seat. "Where do you want to start?"

Chaz adjusted himself in the seat. "Exile. Tell me what happened while you were gone."

"There was nothing but peace and quiet. Crime was still happening, but it was all being handled. Solar was doing a great job. It was much better than what I would have thought he could do in my wildest dreams."

"What about you?"

"I was angry and very spiteful. I was determined not to help even if they needed it. But spite doesn't last long when you're by yourself. Years passed, and nothing changed. They still loved him, and they hated me. I couldn't take it anymore, so I devised a plan. I figured out a way to remove him from the picture while bringing myself back to the forefront. First, I needed to get back into superhero condition. It took a year and half to do all of the necessary training."

"Did it include getting rid of your vices?"

"That was the hardest part. I couldn't let them see me falter, so I had to rely on myself. I pushed all of the women out of my life, all of them. They're too much of a distraction." He gave a half smile.

While Chaz listened to Mr. Marvelous, his thoughts kept throwing his focus. His mind went to his wife. He hasn't talked to her since she left out for work the morning of their argument. *She's not at her parents. Where could she be?* His heart jumped from thoughts of her possibly being harmed somehow. *I hope nothing has happened to her.* At first he felt betrayed from her departure.

She moved her things out while he was gone, without even leaving a 'Dear John' letter. But by this point, he couldn't remember what caused the argument in the first place. All he knew was that he wanted his wife back in his life.

"My coordination and stamina was next," Mr. Marvelous continued. "The rest of the time was used for preparation. It took some time to set everything up. I needed two things: a time when there would be a lot of witnesses and a villain that I could save The City from."

"So you planned on swooping in while Solar was struggling with some villain and save him from a crushing defeat?"

Mr. Marvelous pointed with a mighty smile and bright eyes. "Exactly." He snapped his fingers. "I wanted to show everyone how much better I was and how much they need me."

Chaz's demeanor lifted from seeing his smile. It was like a pat on the head or receiving a gold star. "What kind of training did you do?"

Mr. Marvelous shrugged. "I mostly concentrated on changing my habits. For my strength, I worked out like an elite athlete." He stuck out his chest and motioned like he was doing a chest press. "The only real difference was the amount that I did."

"What was the amount?"

"I did thousands—of repetitions a day."

Chaz's eyebrows shot up. "Thousands a day?"

He agreed. "Thousands. It sounds like a lot, but that was the routine, and I'm too powerful to lift a weight once or twice."

"How was it starting back up? Getting over that first couple of weeks..."

"It was the worst part." Mr. Marvelous shook his head. "But by the end, I was in the best shape of my life."

"So you were ready?"

"Almost." Mr. Marvelous pointed at the photo album.

Chaz picked it up and opened it to the first section. On each page was one picture of Mr. Marvelous. One was from before his training, and the other was after. In each picture, he stood in front of a body length mirror, holding a twin lens reflex camera to his stomach. He looked quite different in each photo. His blotchy and pale skin had turned smooth, clear, and sun-kissed. His eyes looked clearer and more focused. He looked like he had lost at least fifteen pounds.

He wore the same outfit in both, but the second picture looked much cleaner. It was as clean as the first day it was stitched together. The blue 'M' that covered his sternum almost glowed like it was lit by a black light.

"Next, I switched out my suit," he continued. "It needed to be clean like my new personality, and the previous one was well worn. Cleanliness and appearance are both important to me." He motioned his hands over his body to show off his clothes. He was back to looking like the first day they met. Everything he had on from his gloves to his boots were pristine. "Clothing makes the man—as they say." He gave another half-smile.

*Clothes do make the man.* That thought brought Chaz back to his best friend, Mark. He didn't think Mark understood, but he could tell Mr. Marvelous did. Hard work is important to Chaz too, but a person's appearance is how the world will see them and treat them. *No one respects dirty vagrants. They might get a dollar or two periodically, but people don't want to be around them. If you dress like a million bucks, people will treat you like a million bucks. Who doesn't want to be treated with respect?* The argument struck at the core of their beliefs. Both, Chaz and Mark, had their foundations laid by the most influential people in their respective lives while they were still impressionable children.

Chaz's Grandfather, Papa Bobby, would come to their house every day to bring him breakfast and walk him to school. Every day, rain, sleet, or snow, he would arrive on time and dressed to impress. He would tell Chaz about his time in the navy. He was a military hero, and he was Chaz's hero even through his early years of collecting clippings of Mr. Marvelous. Then one day in middle school, Papa Bobby didn't show up. His parents told him what happened; Papa Bobby had a heart attack on his way to pick Chaz up for school. He collapsed several blocks from their house. A young Chaz couldn't understand how something like that could happen. His Grandfather always looked so healthy and lively throughout those years.

Mark's example was his parents. Growing up he watched as they struggled to pay the bills and to keep paying clients coming to the family's business. If they had any money left over, they would put it towards their yearly vacation. As Mark got older, much like his school peers, he would ask for expensive items for presents. They would say, "if it's not broke, then you don't need a new one, and if it is broke, fix it. Money is time, and time is something you can't get back. What you spend your time on should be important and not items you'll throw away a couple of days later."

Chaz frowned as he thought about his friend. Mark, like Tracy, hasn't been taking his calls. *I didn't do anything wrong.* His ego repeated that statement over and over, but it didn't make him feel any better.

"What's wrong? You've gotten quiet all of a sudden."

"I'm sorry. I was thinking about my friend."

"Your friend?" Mr. Marvelous' eyes narrowed.

"We had somewhat of a falling out recently."

Mr. Marvelous stared at him for a few moments, still as a rock. "You told him about me?"

Immediately, Chaz's brow began to sweat, and his heart gave two quick thumps. He cleared his throat before a hard swallow. "No..."

"You don't have to lie." A thin smile stretched across Mr. Marvelous' face. "Relax." Those words brought no relief for Chaz. He felt the adrenaline that coursed through his veins with every rapid pump of his heart. Goosebumps popped up from all of his exposed skin. "True," Mr. Marvelous resumed, "you broke one of the rules, but—I knew about that long ago." His smile now exposed the majority of his white teeth. They were too white.

Chaz turned from away Mr. Marvelous as he pondered the revelation, knowing he wouldn't be able to control his face at the moment. *Does he really know? No. How would he know that?*

"How do I know that?"

Chaz's mouth jerked from the question. *He does know. How? How does he know?* Chaz thought back to his times at Reed's with Mark. *How could he know?* He nervously tapped his foot. Jessica. *Did she tell him about that day?*

"I know the same way I know everything else."

Chaz's thoughts abruptly stopped. He looked at Mr. Marvelous with a face as blank as his mind.

"Ha! You'll need more than that to hide your emotions from me." Mr. Marvelous floated up out of his seat. His feet landed on the ground as quiet as a whisper in space. "I will explain everything, but first, you need to relax." He walked toward the windows. Each step was firm and fluid. He moved with the ease of a man not truly affected by gravity. The floor creaked with each step and shift in weight. He cuffed his hands behind his back. "Relax, Chaz," Mr. Marvelous said in a soothing tone. He took in a deep breath, slow and steady, and then let out an audible exhale. "Just like that."

The smelled of water and rust swept through the room. Chaz's hands felt wet. He looked at them, rubbing his fingers together. "What do you mean?" His question came out choppy from his quick breathing. Chaz closed his eyes and consciously slowed down his breathing. His nose flared with each breath. He flexed his fingers and toes to help with circulation to his extremities. With each breath, he breathed deeper and slower than the last. Once he managed to get himself under somewhat control, he repeated his question. "What do you mean?"

"Today is our last day together Chaz. I would be remiss if I didn't go all the way with this." Mr. Marvelous smiled with closed lips. It was a pleasant smile, much different from the others that Chaz had seen so far. Mr. Marvelous closed the glass balcony doors and drew the curtains closed, one at a time. They slid across the metal rod with a high pitched scrape. The cotton curtains were so thick and heavy that only a minuscule amount of light pierced through.

Nothing could be seen in the room except Mr. Marvelous' silhouette. The next moment, Mr. Marvelous was by the door flipping on a light switch. A flickering incandescent bulb brought light back into the room, brightening the apartment back to what it once was. Almost like a flash on as camera or a strobe light, each pulse reveled the room in its stillness.

Starting around the light, the ceiling began to peel toward the walls. The pieces of the shedding ceiling fell like fluffy snow or lose feathers with each pulse of the bulb. Then, the tops of the pale white walls dripped down to the floor like hot candle wax, heavy and opaque. Mr. Marvelous, who was still standing by the door, faded gradually into the background as the room became dimmer by the second.

The surroundings gradually shrank with the light. They sulked inch by inch, closer to Chaz, closing in on him like a tomb. He watched, transfixed, while trying to control his breathing. The wood floor cracked and split. Chunks of wood dropped into the abyss of darkness that shrouded the floor. He tried to escape and evacuate the room with little success. He called out for Mr. Marvelous, for anyone really, to come and save him, but no sound ever left his mouth. He was stuck, alone, and unable to move his limbs or even blink. It was like he had sleep paralysis but without being asleep. If only he was asleep, then he could wake up, and life would be back to the way it used to be. He wished and begged for a normalcy that would never come.

After the longest and most dreadful ten minutes of his life, the loft had finished transforming. It had morphed into a room that was now the size of an average studio apartment, more or less a quarter of the size of its origin. The new walls that encompassed the place were cracked and stained with splotches of brown mold. The paint peeled in other areas. Chaz instinctively covered his mouth and nose with his shirt. The pin-striped wallpaper that lined the baseboards had rips and scratches. The window in the center of the wall on his far right, which became the main source of light, was covered with old newspaper. Tinges of yellow flared out from the centers of the paper from the effects of sunlight, time, and oxidation. The floor was no longer polished wood but a green and gray carpet with thick patches of grime. Everything in the room looked like it had a horrid odor, but nothing truly stood out. It all smelled like a combination of sweat and ointments.

Chaz looked down at the photo album that sat in his lap since earlier in the day. It was the same album that he had looked through over all of those days. Its leather bound cover had the same cracks and scuffs, but inside was different. The first page had six pictures of various sizes on each side. All of the photos were of people and animals. The animal pictures were of dogs, cats, birds, and other pets. In the group photos, the people sat huddled together with their perfect smiles and clothes. They were all too perfect. Family photos are staged, but they were too perfect. Nobody is ever that happy all of the time. At least one of them should have a child acting up or looking the wrong way.

A rustling sound caught his attention. In front of him was a dark blue curtain that cut the room in almost half. It hung from metal rings like it was clinging on for dear life. He heard a faint voice from behind it.

"This is the truth." The voice quivered with each word.

Chaz stood. The chair, rusted and lopsided, rocked to the right without Chaz's weight to stabilize it. Its seat and back cushions were matching flower prints that covered the catalogs of Papa Bobby's heyday. He casted the album across the room toward the door. The album whacked against the floor. Pictures burst forth from the impact. He yanked open the curtain with both hands, tearing a portion in the process.

There he was, Mr. Marvelous, as helpless and bedridden as a sickly ninety-year-old man. He was bald like a vulture with thick square bifocals and wrinkles that created hills of skin on his face and hands. He reminded Chaz of his grandfather after his second heart attack, frail and helpless on his death bed. Chaz's fists tightened, forcing blood from his palms. His nails were on the brink of piercing his skin. He wanted to punch him right in his stupid old face; one good time, with all of his might. Maybe the hit would be enough to break his nose or launch his glasses across the room. But, Chaz couldn't bring himself to do it, not after seeing Mr. Marvelous like that. His hands loosened. *Mark would've done it.*

Mr. Marvelous smiled, exposing his scattered, coffee stained, jagged teeth. "I'm glad you changed your mind." His voice was shaky with a hint of something else. There was a whistle like quality with some of his words. "Please, sit down. Let me finish the story."

Chaz scowled at the request. He was ready to walk out, leaving Mr. Marvelous and his story behind. *Maybe this was a mistake. I shouldn't have come here.* He looked back at the chair. *What do I have to lose? Only more time.* He looked back again. Reluctantly, Chaz walked back over to the chair and sat down. "You have been bullshitting me this whole time?"

"Well...No. I gave you what you wanted."

"I wanted the truth." He pointed. "You told me you would tell me the truth."

"No." Mr. Marvelous shook his head. "You wanted Mr. Marvelous and everything you dreamt about when you were younger. So I showed you what you wanted to see. You didn't like my smile, so I changed it. You didn't like the layout, so I changed it. I did the same for my appearance."

*Mark was right. I should've listened to him.*

"And no, this is not the same thing Mark was saying." He waved his hand. "This is completely different."

"How is this different? You've been pretending to get me to feel a certain way." He paused. His eyebrows tightened together. "How do you even know about that? How do you keep knowing these things? How is any of this happening?"

He cleared his throat before speaking. "I'm telepathic—with some telekinesis abilities."

Chaz's breathing shortened, eyes widened. "You can read minds too?" A tingling sensation started at his digits and crept up his arms. "How long have you been reading my mind?"

"It's more like listening to a radio." He tapped his ear. "Sometimes it's like a television."

"How long?"

Mr. Marvelous tilted his head to the side.

"How long?" Chaz demanded.

"Since I can remember. It's all I could ever do," he said. "Look at me. Do I look like I have super human strength or super speed?"

Chaz's clenched his teeth, straining his crowns. "How long have you been reading my mind?" He roared.

"Since the first day you came and every day since," Mr. Marvelous explained. "Everything else—all of it was illusions. Just like what you've seen these past days."

"Illusions? The room...has it always looked like this?"

"Yes. I had to do it."

Chaz shook his head and fold his arms. His lip curled as he frowned.

"You know it's true."

"No." He glared.

"Think about it Chaz. If you would have seen me like this on our first meeting, would you have believed me to be Mr. Marvelous?"

Chaz's brow furrowed as he thought about it. He looked down, fumbled with his fingers. "I would have thought you were a fraud."

"You would have left before hearing me out. Nothing I would've showed or told would have convinced you."

*He's right. I would have left and moved on to a new story.* He got paid by the story, and its impact, not by unsubstantiated gossip. There were always new stories for Chaz to report on at the paper and wasting his time on something that he couldn't prove would've put him in the poor house.

It would also be plain ol' disappointing seeing some old man trying to use Mr. Marvelous' name to become popular. He could never let anyone sully Mr. Marvelous' reputation, but it was him. He really met Mr. Marvelous, the hero who saved The City multiple times. *He defeated so many to protect us all and then became the biggest celebrity we have ever known, only to ruin his own reputation with drugs, alcohol, pride, and violence.*

"You would have left and moved on to a new story. Am I right?"

Chaz nodded.

"So what is a few illusions to make sure that this great moment would happen?"

*Few illusions...* Chaz's mind drifted off to all of the stories Mr. Marvelous had told him so far. Every memory he recalled of his time with Mr. Marvelous and his exploits were followed up with lingering thoughts from his last day with Mark. *'That guy is playing you.'*

"I only did what I had to do to convince you to stay. That's it."

*'He got what he got because of himself.'* Chaz's face shifted back to disdain. "It was you all along," he said.

"Excuse me?" Mr. Marvelous tilted his head.

"It was you. You created your own downfall. Those booze and drugs must have affected your illusions. Am I right?"

Mr. Marvelous sulked.

"They might have gotten you hooked, but all it did was expose you for who you really were."

"No. I changed when I started using them. I truly did..."

Chaz's eyes lit up. "What about all of your fights?" He began to grimace. "Dr. Charge and Positron? Killer Gorilla? Dynamo? Scorch? Was any of them real?"

"That's complicated."

*'Stop acting like a politician.'* "It isn't." Chaz violently shook his head. "It's an easy question. Were they real or not?"

"Yes." He paused, twisting his upper body to face Chaz better. "They were all real. All of them. Real people, doing real crimes."

Chaz's body relaxed. He felt relief from Mr. Marvelous' response. After all of the bombshells of lies being dropped throughout this session, the truth was like a cease fire, and Chaz was a soldier climbing out of his foxhole.

"They just—didn't have all of those abilities."

Just that quick, Chaz regretted coming out of his foxhole only to be shot at once more. "They didn't have the abilities? What does that mean?"

"Listen. They were bad people, and I brought them to justice."

"You faked their powers? Why would you fake that?"

"Let me finish the story."

"How can I even trust the rest?"

"You know what I am saying is the truth. You already knew most of the stories. I'm just giving you a new perspective and more of the details."

"I thought I knew the truth," Chaz snapped.

"Constantly being a skeptic doesn't make you smart because you've never been tricked with pseudo knowledge. It just leaves your mind full of doubt and empty of facts," Mr. Marvelous said, stern as an overbearing professor.

What Mr. Marvelous said made sense to him. It was the same as Mark's opinion but said in a more eloquent way. Chaz respected that. And because of that respect, he decided to give Mr. Marvelous the time to finish his story. "Ok. Tell me the rest."

Mr. Marvelous smiled. "I'm glad you changed your mind. Now, where did we leave off?"

Chaz threw his hands up to the question. "I don't remember. A lot has happen since then."

Both of them looked up and to the right as they tried to rewind back to the point. All of the stress and revelations have made thinking back that far more difficult than it should have been. At the same time, both of them remembered.

"The outfit makes the man," they said.

"Right after you gave me that photo album with your sample pictures," Chaz added.

Mr. Marvelous looked disappointed by Chaz's quibble. "All of those pictures were either destroyed or lost over the years."

*He's lying.* "Right." Chaz's upper lip twitched.

"That night I set the rest of my plan in motion. It hinged on having the hero fight someone I knew he couldn't beat. That way I could swoop in and save the day like I used to."

"But that would mean..." His eyes widen. *The Maestro.*

"I released The Maestro from his cell in hopes that he would defeat the hero."

Chaz's heart stopped. His stomach twisted up in knots.

"I knew that none of his gadgets were capable of stopping The Maestro or his brood. Even if he could figure out The Maestro's secret, it would be too many of them and that would leave me to clean things up. I planned on arriving to the scene right before Solar was executed and then beat The Maestro with ease. None of that worked out at all. There were critter bodies all over the place. I found him and The Maestro laying on the ground next to each other, lifeless. Solar had dried blood that had spewed from his mouth, all over his face, and semisolid blue fluid on both of his outstretched arms. One of The Maestro's arms was lodged in Solar's abdomen up to its wrist. His carcass stared at The Maestro with wide, veiny, bulging eyes. The Maestro body was mangled; legs ensnared by a rope, enormous charcoal eyes had been impaled by Solar's thumbs, daggers and glass poked through the rest of ITs face and chest."

"Are you serious?" Chaz's heart raced, seemingly taking up residence in his throat. His hands and feet were a winter's night cold. He tasted bile on the back of his tongue.

"You don't know what happened?"

Chaz shook his head. "No, no, no, no." He rocked in the chair. Chaz covered his face with his balled up fists, supporting the weight of his head with his elbows. "I feel sick."

"I can help you with that," Mr. Marvelous said with a gentle smile.

"Help?" Chaz peered from behind his hands. "Don't you fucking dare."

Mr. Marvelous leaned back from the insult. His eyes narrowed and lips tightened.

"You let that monster out," Chaz continued. "You're out of your mind. Hundreds of people could have been killed."

"Nobody died, I made sure of that. I just wasn't expecting that outcome."

"Well, the hero died, was that apart of your plan too?"

"Never. I just wanted him to get roughed up a little. Their fight happened too fast, which threw off my timing. By the time I got there, the fight was over.

"You told me you didn't know where the military took The Maestro."

"I didn't know," he hacked, clearing his throat, "at first. I found out about a year later. They told me where The Maestro was and the kind of experiments they were performing."

*He lied again. He didn't tell you everything because he knew how it would sound.*

"And you don't?" Mr. Marvelous questioned.

"What?"

"You're being a hypocrite."

"A hypocrite?" Chaz looked around the room. *He's not talking about me.*

"When you and your wife had this discussion, you were on my side."

"Don't compare an argument I had with my wife to what you did. I forgot to tell her what I was doing. You," Chaz thrusted his finger forward, "almost got people killed just so you could be popular."

"Did you really forget?"

"Yes...I thought I told her."

"And I've always told you the truth. Did I leave somethings out? Yes, but it added to the story."

"What in the world is wrong with you?"

"Nothing—and nothing is wrong with you."

"We are not the same. I don't go around lying to thousands of people for some fame. You could've accomplished all of the same things without the trickery."

"After the first time, I couldn't go back to normal. The ball had already started rolling. I had to keep feeding a fire that I probably shouldn't have started in the first place."

"What about The Maestro?" He questioned. "None of the villains had powers right? So why would they still have 'IT' contained if The Maestro abilities were all illusions too?"

Mr. Marvelous stared with nothing to reveal behind his eyes. He was as empty as a new book.

"Was The Maestro real?" Chaz shouted.

Mr. Marvelous' body jumped a little. "Yes."

"This is unbelievable." He tapped his knuckles against his forehead. "I keep trying to see the positive in this. I keep trying and trying to understand your side, but—I can't see it." He clinched his teeth, abrading his jeans with his hands. His hands burned from the rubbing, but he didn't stop. "What you've done is wrong. You put hundreds, no," he shook his head, "thousands of people's lives in danger just so you could look cool."

"I know." He nodded. "I thought my plan would get me back to where I once was. I wanted the respect. I wanted the love." He sat up, supporting himself on one elbow. His head resting on his shoulder. "I made the wrong choice. In his death, he became an eternal sentinel for The City and a shining symbol of heroism and integrity. They erected a statue for him in The Square. That should have been my figure out there, standing tall for all to see. I should be the one that is celebrated." He paused for a moment, to calm himself down. "I was angry before, but after the statue, I felt hurt and betrayed."

*He betrayed us. He was jealous.*

"The Maestro," Mr. Marvelous continued, "was The City's last villain. That was my last chance, and I blew it. Forty years later, here I am, and there you are. Time changes a man. I have lived through the extreme highs that made me arrogant and jaded. Then, I fell into a deep abyss which cultivated fear and anger. These past forty years have given me nothing but solitude. I have learned from my mistakes," he said. "So that's why I have brought you here. I know I have made mistakes, but I have paid for them. I hope that with my story finally being told I could be forgiven by the citizens of The City and maybe—finally forgive myself.

"But why? Before all of this, I knew more about you than most people, and I still had hope in you. Now they will know even more. Why do you think they will forgive you?"

"I don't know." Mr. Marvelous fell back onto his bed. "I want them to forgive me." He took a deep breath and looked up at the ceiling. "I'm dying Chaz, and I don't want to die like this. I don't want to die alone." His voice quivered. "I don't want to die being hated. I don't want to be forgotten. I don't have anyone. I never had any children, no real relationship to speak of." His blood shot eyes overflowed with tears. They pour down the side of his face in a constant stream. "Ever since Ms. Ambers and I, I had been avoiding companionship, but I've always wanted it. I've starved for it."

*I don't want to die alone.* Chaz thought about his wife again. He thought about his best friend. They were his deepest connections. They helped to keep him grounded, and now both of those connections were on the brink of breaking. He'd strained their relationships ever since he met Mr. Marvelous. Maybe it started before then. The destination became more important than the journey and the people he was traveling with. He kept pushing forward, never looking back at or checking on his companions.

They fell behind and he kept walking, until one day he looked up and he was by himself in the wilderness, helpless against an ambush from life's difficulties. It was a cold path that he walked. It was a path that Mr. Marvelous himself had walked too. He was decades further along, so his footprints were fading, but they were there.

"It might be too late for that now," he sniffed. "but I thought that maybe—we could be friends after all of this." He wiped his eyes several times, but the tears kept coming, rewetting the areas that he had dried. "You were the only one that still believed in me." Mr. Marvelous turned to look at Chaz. His lips quaked as he spoke. "You saw the good in me and most of the actions I committed."

Chaz's throat tightened. He blinked several times to clear his watery eyes. He was beginning to understand. Mr. Marvelous had been waiting for someone like him to catch up on the path so he didn't have to walk alone anymore. He could finally have at least one person for company as he approached death.

"I want the rest of the civilians to know that too. I believed you would be the best person to explain it. But, if that didn't happen, I still wanted us to be friends. I've been alone for a long time with no one to talk to or laugh with. My memories had been the only things to keep me company. Some of those memories are exceptional, yet the ones that replayed the most were all of the mistakes I have made." He wiped his eyes again. This time leaving his hands to cover his face. "I was the reason I was alienated. I know that," he sobbed. "I'm sorry. I don't know what else to do. I can't bring Solar back. I can't change any of my actions." His words are almost drowned out by his wailing.

Chaz couldn't take it anymore. He walked over to Mr. Marvelous, took one of his hands, and he patted it. "I will finish what I started," he whispered. "I swear."

Embarrassed, Mr. Marvelous covered his face up with his free arm. "Thank you."

"No, thank you. Thank you for everything you have done for me and The City."

"Will I see you again?"

"I don't know." Chaz let go of Mr. Marvelous' hand. "I have some mending to do. It's time for me to look in the mirror and face myself."

"I understand." He gave a sad smile. It was a smile that hoped Chaz would change his mind. "You can't change what you did, but in time, you can change yourself." He winked.

Chaz smiled back. "I'll keep that in mind." He walked toward the door for the last time, his head hung low. The photo album leaned upright against the door. He picked it up and flipped through the pages. He didn't bother to grab up the loose pictures that fell when he chucked the album toward the door.

"You can keep it. Think of it as a souvenir." The album was empty except for one picture on the very last page. It was a picture of Mr. Marvelous in his first costume, smiling from ear to ear. "It's real." Mr. Marvelous added.

Chaz looked at it for a moment. He thought about leaving it behind with Mr. Marvelous, the docks, and everything else that has forced its way into his life since the first meeting. He thought about stuffing the picture in his pocket and carrying it around with him until the story was published, only to bring it back to Mr. Marvelous once it was all over. "Thank you, again." He tucked the album under his arm. He couldn't let an opportunity like that pass him by.

"My name—I didn't tell you my name yet. It's..."

Chaz stopped halfway out of the door. Mr. Marvelous smiled, waiting for him to turn around.

"It's your secret identity. A secret isn't a secret if it is told." With that last remark, Chaz left out of Mr. Marvelous life, closing the door on their meetings, never to see him again.

# CHAPTER TWELVE

## Editorial

That was the last day I saw him, the great Mr. Marvelous. He could defeat everything but time itself.

I tried to tell his story the best way I could, and I think I have succeeded. Over his active years, he has been the savior of many lives and also the chaotic element of many more. But, for forty years, he has punished himself. Granted, the shock of his revelations almost caused me to go against my standards. There were times where I was ready to get up and leave, but as the story went on, I began to see myself. People do bad things and some of them regret it. For others, it takes our legal system to show them the right path. But for this hero, there were no jails that could hold him, and there were no authority figures to enforce their laws upon him. He didn't have a mentor to guide him or to teach him the proper way to live. He was unique and powerful; captivating and awe-inspiring, but he was also reckless, impulsive, aggressive, and domineering. He was more than us. He did much more than we could ever hope to achieve in two lifetimes, and that is precisely why what he did stood out to me. It takes a strong individual to not only realize that they're wrong and at fault, but to also punish themselves for their misdeeds.

So that's what he did. He accepted his exile from The City and lived his life in almost complete seclusion from the civilians that he once protected; only receiving help from a few individuals when his worsening health became too much to handle on his own.

In the end, I was picked by this remarkable hero to tell his story, and that's what I have done. It was a challenging experience. But now, I am compelled to do one last thing. One last favor to somehow pay back my childhood inspiration for all of the acts that he did throughout his crime fighting career. I would like everyone who has read through this article to consider his life as their own. Think about the mistakes you have made in your life for personal gain or from a lack of empathy. Take a moment to think about all of the times you sat back and watched some injustice happen, the times you might have stolen, cheated, or attacked another individuals. What if you were the one that was ostracized by your community? What if it was you that saved thousands and helped to maintain order in your community only to be considered a black sheep for being involved in a few taboo incidents? I want you to really think about that to yourself.

After forty long years, wouldn't you want to be forgiven too?


"That's it," Jessica said, sitting in a metal chair beside his bed. "Did you like it?" She leaned over and placed two fingers on his throat, checking his heart rate.

"Yes," he whispered. "I loved every word."

"That's good." She patted him on his chest. "Could you imagine—being able to meet Mr. Marvelous?"

His face quivered as he smiled at her.

"Do you think any of that is true?"

"The paper hasn't lied to me yet," He said.

She laughed. "You can never tell now-a-days. There are so many fake stories going around. The other day I read about this reporter, Jacob Stienburg, or Stiener—"

"Jackson Steward?" He interjected.

"Yes, Jackson Steward. Have you heard about this story?"

He shook his head.

"Mr. Steward was a celebrated anchor for the KRP news show, Headlines, in Foxglove; that man was outed as a fraud. He wrote a book about his time in captivity by Ethiopian pirates. I know it's not the same as the papers but..."

He raised his eyebrows.

"All of it was made up," she continued. "Can you believe that? He was living in Chicago at the time. He wrote that he was kidnapped and was being held for ransom." She threw up her hands. They flopped back down to the chair's armrests. "I mean, can you believe it? The nerve of that guy."

He tucked his lips and shook his head. He looked around the room.

"He made a public apology, but he shouldn't have been able to keep his job. Fame makes everything better I guess." She paused for a moment. "Hey." She caught him off guard. His body tensed up from the alarm. "Didn't you live here while Mr. Marvelous was around? How did he act?"

"Mr. Marvelous?" He sat up and shifted his weight against the wall. "He was a firecracker." He smiled. "A shooting star in the night's sky." He picked up a cup from the over-the-bed table, taking a sip of the water. "I met him in person once."

"Really..." She playfully tapped him on the arm. "What happened?"

"It was really quick. Nothing to write home about."

"Oh, stop being so tight lipped," Jessica said while pouting.

He coughed into his hand. "You remind me of my niece when you do that." He reached over to pinch her cheek. She grabbed up his incoming hand and pulled it down to her lap.

"Please..." She squeezed his hand.

"All right, Jessica."

She smiled and bounced around in her seat.

"We had a blizzard that year. It was the biggest one I had ever seen, at the time, in my twelve years of life. The snow came up to my knees where it wasn't plowed. I was sent by my mother to go get a couple of things from the local drug store. Most of the streets were plowed, lucky for me, but during those times The City didn't use salt."

Jessica's face twisted up from the revelation.

"A car careened over the hill." He motioned his hand like a speedy snake.

"Oh no..." She held her own hand. "He was fishtailing?"

He laughed and then changed his hand movement to more of a tail fin. "It wasn't a steep hill, but he had a hard time stopping, regardless." He reached over and tapped her knee. "Car brakes back then didn't work too well on a sunny day." After a quick smile, he continued the story. "At the same time, a beautiful young woman," he smiled as he reflected back on her image, "layered in her winter clothes, edged her way across the street at the bottom of the hill. She took her time with each step, trying not to slip or fall," he said. "Once the driver noticed the young woman, he pounded on the horn to warn her. People came out from the other stores to see what was going on. It was a quiet area—at the time. I stood at the corner, directly across from her, holding on to a brown paper bag. I didn't know what to do. I was terrified of what was going to happen next." He took another sip of water. "She let out a harrowing shriek when she saw the car coming. She tried to run, but her feet slipped on some black ice in the middle of the road. She collapsed to her hands and knees."

Jessica covered her mouth, dampening the gasp that leapt from out of her.

"That's when Mr. Marvelous showed up. It was a sight to see." His dark hazel eyes grew bright. "He floated down from the sky right in front of the car, as light as a snowflake. He caught the car with both hands. It jerked a little but it stayed in place. Everyone cheered. The woman, still on her hand and knees, was lifted up by Mr. Marvelous and dropped off right beside me."

Jessica gave a silent clap, grinning from ear to ear.

"That's how I was smiling."

She tapped him on the arm.

"After he moved the car and spoke to the driver, he took some time to talk all of the bystanders that gathered. He even rubbed my head. He said it was for good luck." He perched his lips, his eyebrows dropped woefully. "And then he was off..." He whistled as he motioned his free hand up towards the ceiling. "Back into the sky and to another part of The City."

"Nothing to gossip over?" She tapped him on the arm again. "They should've interviewed you for a story."

"No, I couldn't."

"You wouldn't want to be in the papers?"

"They don't need me when they can get it from the horse's mouth." He swatted in front of his face. "I leave all that fame for Mr. Marvelous."

Jessica nodded and smiled. She stood up with a moan while she stretched. "Time to hit the road." She sighed.

"Will you be back tomorrow?"

"Of course." She stooped down and picked up her sling backpack that leaned against the foot of his bed. "As long as you need me, I will be right here." She smiled and slipped the bag over her shoulder. She clicked the plastic buckle into place. "You don't have to worry about me. Will I see you tomorrow?"

"God willing and the creek don't rise," he said cheerfully.

"Good day, sir."

"Have a good night, Jessica."

Jessica patted down her chest and thighs. She looked around the room before looking at the front of her bag. "Oh, there it is." Her ID dangled from the strap.

He laid back on the bed and looked up at the ceiling. Two out of four of the lights in the ceiling fan were dead. He had been meaning to get those replaced.

"Do you want me to turn out the light before I leave?" Jessica said standing in the doorway.

"No, I've got it." He clapped twice and the lights went out. The moon's light crashed into the room through a solitary window. It was full and bright.

"Good day."

"Good night."

Jessica gently closed the door behind her. It was late, and she didn't want to make too much noise in the hallway; some of the other residents were very light sleepers. She pulled on the strap to make it more comfortable for her breasts, before walking down the hallway toward the staircase. The floor felt like it was moving, and she was being dragged along. Halfway down the hallway, Jessica stumbled to the side, catching herself on the nearest wall. Her shoulder bumped against the wall. The wall lamp above her flickered from the impact before becoming stable again. Her head throbbed. She squeezed her eyes shut from the pain.

Jessica didn't move until the buzzing in her head stopped. It was a loud continuous pitch that subsided as her equilibrium came back. She reopened her eyes. Her vision still blurry from squeezing them shut. She looked down at the floor to avoid most of the light. Her shoes came into focus. The heel's tip had broken off of her right foot. She used her arm to prop herself up as she took off both of her heels. Her purse swung loosely on her arm from its strap.

She stretched and flexed her toes in the carpet, relieving the pain from them being confined in her heels for too long. Before walking down the stairs, she groomed herself; checked for lint, combed her shoulder length hair, buttoned up her blouse, and straightened her mini skirt. She tucked the heels under her arm and carefully descended down the stairs, holding onto the wooden rail to avoid falling. The mini skirt restricted her movement and the stockings she wore didn't aid her in traction on the thin carpet.

Two more claps sounded in the darkness before the lights flashed back on, much brighter than before. It had been an hour since Jessica had left the apartment. The grizzled old man looked over at the newspaper sitting in the chair. Jessica left it there after getting up from the seat.

He tossed the covers off of his body in one quick motion. They flopped to the side. He took in a deep breath, and swung his feet off the side. Two empty prescription bottles fell out of the bed and hit the floor the same time as his feet. The floor's tile was cold and smooth. He took another deep breath before standing. His bones cracked and popped as he reached his full height. He picked up the paper, skimming over the article, folded it, and stuck the paper under his arm.

He waddled his way to the bathroom that was next to the head of the bed, a pair of black sheer panties hung from the door knob. The bathroom was much colder than the rest of the apartment. Goosebumps formed on his bare arms. He turned on the sink's hot water. The pipes knocked and moaned as the water approached. He braced himself on the sides of the sink, conserving his energy for the upcoming long process. The medicine cabinet mirror fogged up from the steam. He dipped a washcloth in the scolding water, wrung out the excess, and placed it over his face.

# MAGNANIMOUS ABSOLUTION

He strolled out of the bathroom, cleanly shaven, and refreshed from his mini sauna. His loose skin was now firm and smooth as a teenager. He took a couple of quick steps over to the small window, a thin layer of dust covered its sill and pane. The moon's fullness and beauty eclipsed everything else that could be seen through the glass. He stared into its light like a child with a television, unblinking. He reached out, as if he could somehow hold that spinning, gray rock in his hands, and keep it for himself.

He stepped closer with his arms out stretched. His hands bumped into the glass, it rippled with the surrounding wall from the impact. The ripples cascaded outward like a lake's stillness, broken by a tossed rock. He flung both hands apart, sliding the moon and previously invisible curtains to the side. Behind them were three floor-to-ceiling windows, crystal clear.

The orange glow from the rising sun dissolved his pajamas, starting at his bare feet, exposing the white and blue leather costume underneath. His gloves squeaked as he opened the main window's French doors and stepped out onto the stone balcony.

A cool breeze blew in toward the docks from the harbor. His jet black hair fluttered in the wind. Seagulls circled above the Loft's parking lot, eyeing the scattered pieces of bread. Mr. Marvelous basked in the sun's rays for a few minutes. It warmed his skin like an electric blanket. He watched as the cargo ships and other nautical crafts cruised in and out of the harbor.

He looked down at the newspaper in his hand, finally noticing the title; 'Magnanimous Absolution'. He smirked at the irony and then crushed the pages into a ball, tossing it to the side. A strong wind swooped in and carried it away from the balcony. Its contents dispersed over The Loft's courtyard. His body shook as he laughed to himself before looking up to the partly cloudy sky.

211

"Everyone loves an underdog." Levitating off of the ground, he darted up through the atmosphere, punching a hole through several clouds. The air cracked as he flew toward the sea.

\*\*\*

Thank you for reading my debut novel, **Magnanimous Absolution**. Please leave a review for the novel at the place of purchase or any other book review site.

Be on the look out for my upcoming works in the near future.

Made in the USA
Middletown, DE
27 August 2020